Lilli J Wettke

656 days

The story of a girl who survived

AF191537

Lilli J Wettke

656 days
The story of a girl who survived

Impressum

Bibliografische Information der Deutschen Nationalbibliothek: Die Deutsche Nationalbibliothek verzeichnet diese Publikation in der Deutschen Nationalbibliografie; detaillierte bibliografische Daten sind im Internet über http://dnb.dnb.de abrufbar.

Lektorat: Julia Deutsch, Lilli J Wettke
Korrektorat: Lilli J Wettke

Verlag: BoD · Books on Demand GmbH, Überseering 33, 22297 Hamburg, bod@bod.de

Druck: Libri Plureos GmbH, Friedensallee 273, 22763 Hamburg

ISBN: 978-3-8192-7753-5

For all flowers,
that still manage to grow after a forest fire.

About her

The calm before the storm.
She likes to look at the sea. Often, she just stands there, with
her bare feet in the cold sand and the blowing wind in her
hair. There is a certain smell that heralds the calm before the
storm. The breeze in her nose sounds like the sea's last cry for
help before the storm swallows it. She often sits there, on a
dune, her dune, smelling this very smell and listening to the
sea's painful screams. The sound calms her, gives her a sense
of home, of secrecy. Now she lies there, twisted in herself. Her
body is in most places as blue as the sea. Red blood flows
from her nose and from the cut left by his knife. She had felt
the calm before the storm on her way home, had rejoiced at
the secrecy it gave her. She was bouncing. Only five minutes
to get home.
And now she lies here, an hour later and it is still five minutes
until home. The calm before the storm is gone, for the storm
had broken loose. Now she understood the sea, and why it
was screaming. Now she laid there, left alone. Her trousers
were open, and her shirt stuck to her like a single torn shred.
Five minutes and the calm before the storm would not have
changed its meaning forever. Five minutes and she would
have arrived home safely with the feeling of secrecy in her
heart. But no, he had seen her. He had felt relentless, he had
scoured over her restlessly like the storm over the sea.
It had not mattered to him, for she was only one of the many
seas in which he had beaten his waves, but the sea was now
restless. It kept moving, throwing huge waves. She had the
feeling that she would never again be able to come to rest. She
laid there still from the outside, but her thoughts dragged her
to the bottom of the sea, in a vortex beneath the surface of the
water. She laid there for a long time, until the waves subsided,
leaving a stillness, a stillness of death.

3

What had just been marked by loud noises and deafening rumblings, by man-high waves and metre-deep swirls now laid still, calm, smooth and broken.

Now she also came to know the calm after the storm, and she despaired. Her thoughts appeared again on the surface of the water, but it was too late, she was dead, her thoughts drowned. Yet she lived, lying on the ground as a silent shell, breathing without being alive. The calm after the storm ate her up, for it had nothing familiar. It was nothing but a cruel emptiness left behind by the storm. Now she really understood the sea, and from now on she hated the smell of the calm before the storm, for she had felt the suffering that the sea had to experience.

Josefine

"Actually, how would you react if I kissed you right now?"

In hindsight, this question alone should have thrown me off, but I didn't realise it at that time. Jane and I had been best friends for years, so what intention would this question have other than simple interest. That's why I went into it and replied:
"To be honest, I wouldn't think it was that great! I think friendship should remain friendship and relationship should remain relationship!"
"So, may I kiss you then?" She looked at me cheekily, but also expectantly. Had I not made myself clear enough? I loved Jane, I really did, but only in a platonic manner. I felt uncomfortable on the spot and slipped a little away from her, symbolically, just to be on the safe side. She moved a little closer to me. I felt pressurised, my pulse quickened, I could feel the unease welling up inside me. She wouldn't hurt me; I was aware of that. I knew her well enough to be sure of that by now. She was a good soul, and I knew that she liked me. That's why she would never do anything to harm me. I was completely convinced of that.
"Oh come on! I just want to try it out, don't always be such a killjoy!"
I was seriously starting to feel indisposed. I felt the need to just run away, anywhere. Just away. I didn't want to openly show my insecurity as I didn't want to offend her, so I tried to change the subject as quickly as possible. It didn't work. While I was talking, she kept sliding closer and closer to me until I got up and sat down on the floor. It was a clear sign, but Jane didn't even make a secret out of the fact that she didn't care what I thought about her "idea". Or did she just not realise? Yes, that had to be the case, she didn't notice, otherwise it was

impossible to explain her behaviour. She wasn't usually so slow on the uptake, but I refused to allow myself the thought that she might not care about my boundaries.

I wanted to escape this situation somehow, but how?

Simply asking her to leave my flat would have been rude, and I didn't want her to think that I distrusted her in any way. She was my best friend, and I loved her with all my heart... as a friend. The last thing I wanted to do was offend her, because there was no way I was going to risk what we had. What kind of friend would I be? Our friendship was sacred to me. It was one of a kind, we were different in some ways, but usually that wasn't even a problem. Opposites attract, right?
Us being polar opposites usually was the charm of our relationship, but in situations like this, it was… impractical.

My plan to sit down didn't quite work as intended, because Jane also got up and sat on the floor directly in front of me. She left so little space that our knees were touching. Then she leant forward and...
I put my hand out in front of her and said: "Stop! Stop that! Are you out of your mind? I don't want that!" in such a way that no misunderstandings were possible. I stood up and sat down a foot away. My hands were shaking. I was more or less trapped in the situation, had no way out, like a convict in prison. Jane came after me "Ey, Ey, Ey, calm down. I'm not going to hurt you. Stop being so paranoid! What's going to happen?" I sniggered sheepishly, not knowing how to react. I didn't comment on her behaviour otherwise, what else was there to say, but I consciously made sure that our knees didn't touch this time, just be safe. I didn't want to insinuate anything against my best friend not for all the good in the world...
I should have, and I should have chased her out of my flat, but I couldn't have known at that time.

This game went on a few more times. I tried to have a normal conversation, she came closer to me, I slipped away. I was overwhelmed. I had gotten to know Jane as such a friendly, polite and considerate person.

I wasn't in any position to doubt her at this moment. Why would I? Why would she make a 180 degrees twist in her personality? *Why?*

My doorbell rang. Finally! A chance to take a few breaths. I stood up and opened the door. I was delighted that this situation had been disturbed by whoever angel was currently standing on my doorstep. In my imagination, I would return, and everything would be normal again. In front of me was my neighbour from above. Mid-sixties, no wife, no kids, no grandkids. He was pretty lonely and sometimes searched for someone to talk to. I liked his company, that is why I sometimes had dinner with him.

"Hey, I am so sorry, but I have guests over" I said.

"Well, that's all right… wait, are you okay, dear?" As it sems my confusion about the situation with Jane could be read from my face. I heard Jane move in the living room, which coincidently meant, that she could hear me as well. I would have been honest, but that wasn't a real option now. Wait? Honest about what? There was nothing to lie about. I was meeting up with a dear friend of mine. Jane had her special moments sometimes, so what? The rest was just something my head was too weird to process correctly. Jane told me that nothing was going on, so why couldn't I just trust her?

"Of course I am all right, I hope you are to! I am just a little stressed out with work, that's all"

"Well then, I wouldn't want to inconvenience you any longer"

"Flibbertigibbet, no! You are not inconveniencing me at all. Let's have dinner again in a few days, all right?"

"All right, you have your fun!"

When I entered the living room, it seemed like Jane hadn't come back to her senses after all. Instead, she just decided to update her game and to keep playing. For her, it was nothing more, just a game she enjoyed.

After some time, she managed to trap me into a corner. It reminded me of chess in an odd way. Checkmate!

At this point, I must have said no at least thirteen times, but she didn't want to hear it. With every time, my words became more powerless, less demanding, more pleading. My mind had given into my fate.

She had always been the dominant one, but it had never been like this. I never felt like she used that power she had over me, to dominate me. I tried to get up, but she grabbed me. A wall to my left, a wall to my right, her in front of me, over me. I was trapped. "No" I stuttered one last time. A soulless attempt, a hopeless attempt, I knew it wasn't going to help me in any way.

It wasn't an order any longer, just a begging sound. The kind of sound someone makes, when being held at gunpoint.

She leaned over me further, I tried to stop her, I really did. Jane was stronger than me. She was laying on top of me, her bodyweight pinning me to the ground. It would happen, I knew it, I had to come to peace with this thought.

She slowly started to touch me, and my eyes started to water. Her hand wandered over my boobs until she petted my waist. I thanked every form of grace, that I had changed my outfit last minute. No lowcut top, no short skirt. Her fingers circled over my butt when she kissed my neck, my cheek. Next her hand was on the inside of my lap. My panic had reached its climax, and I was unable to catch a breath. I was out of air, it felt like my lounges were tied up. My heart was racing, I couldn't hold my tears in for any longer. One sole drop of salty liquid left my eye, and with it, my soul.

There was an unknown form of pain in my stomach. My

whole body, every little muscle inside of me was tensed. I felt like I was going to pass out, I felt like I was falling, falling, bursting on the ground. I was dizzy, and yet another tear ran down my cheek. I was falling, and falling, but there was never any ground I could hit, I was infinitely falling.

I didn't want this. I wanted to stay strong; I didn't *want* to cry. I wanted to keep any last bit of dignity I had.

Her tongue was in my mouth, I could taste her without wanting to.

It felt terrible, and these minutes that passed like hours tore me to shreds. It didn't kill me, but something inside me died that day.

Within these seconds something in me withered away, just like a plant who is withheld from the water.

She moved her leg away from my stomach and slowly made our lips part. She didn't hold me down any longer, *she didn't have to.* When I tried to sit, the dizziness got the better of me. But I kept composed, I refused to show any sign of weakness in this moment.

"How did you like it?", Jane asked, her breath hallowing over my skin. The tightening in my stomach morphed into the blank will to vomit.

The ringtone of a mobile phone cut through the silence like a knife. Jane got up and said hello, before leaving the room. The moment she was out of sight I collapsed.

After approximately two minutes, she came back. My posture straightened as I couldn't bear to let her see my weakness.

"Sorry, I have to go!", she said, grabbing her Jacked. I felt tones of weight lifting from my heart.

What she added, let fear crawl down my spine.

"The next time we proceed"

Jane

Soleil had a talent for calling me at the wrong times. There could have been so much more happening between me and Josefine. She always had to find her way of ruining things for me. Who did she think she was?

I didn't love her like I used to in a long time.

To be precise, I was annoyed by her constant happy, energetic attitude. I couldn't bare her presence any longer.

In the beginning I really adored her, but by now I thought of her as unbearable.

I didn't even find her attractive anymore. Not, since she got this huge mandala tattoo on her shoulder. She designed it herself. I told her not to get it inked, but she wouldn't listen. She said she liked the motive, and she wanted people to see her personality, just by looking at the art on her skin. Sounded like something Josefine would say. Both of them were pathetic, only that I loved Josefine.

I didn't love Soleil anymore, but I also wasn't about to break up with her, as that would have been fairly stupid. She was my professor's daughter, and god he adored her.

So I decided to just meet other woman that I actually found alluring behind her back instead. And by woman, I meant Josefine.

Soleil

Had I done something wrong? Jane had seemed unhappy about my call. I had immediately asked if everything was all right, but she had said yes. I couldn't figure her out lately. Something had changed between us, but I didn't know what it was. Jane wasn't as affectionate as she used to be in the beginning. Somehow all my attempts to refresh our relationship left her cold. I felt quite abandoned because I had the impression that she was avoiding me. She wouldn't even take my hand when we were out together. I had already tried to address the issue several times because I felt that communication was always the most important thing in a relationship. She had always quickly changed the subject when I brought up my concerns, so I really was out of ideas on what I should do. She always made up excuses that sounded nothing like her, *nothing like the woman I fell so madly in love with.*

Josefine

When I heard the door close behind Jane, I finally let out a
sigh of relief. I let the shaking- that I had suppressed with all
my power, take over me. I was unable to move any longer. My
fingers became cold and stiff, my heartrate was around three
times as high as would have been healthy.
I was shaking, still I felt sweat building on my forehead and
suddenly, I also felt trouble breathing. My ribcage felt like it
was way too small, like it was about to burst. My lounges
burned like I just sprinted trough a marathon. I gasped.
Everything in me tightened. The pain in my soul was so
strong that it effected my whole body. I was at the verge of
crying, of screaming in pain. My head moved into an up looking position, I fought for breath. I opened my mouth to let out
a scream, but there was no sound, I was mute. I silently
screamed out all the suffering that had built up inside me. I
screamed, but it was silent, so nobody noticed.

Suddenly everything was gone, all the pain, all these feelings
had left me as if they had exited through my open mouth.
I only felt half human anymore. I felt like every inch of hu-
manity inside me had been blown away.
My being on this earth was nothing more than an empty,
numb, callous shell of human flesh.
I did not feel anything anymore. I wanted to cry, but I was unable to. My body had given up all his function. Only the ag-
ony of breathing was still mine.
I was a stone on the ground of a frozen lake, cold, stiff, hard…
blunted, completely free from any form of human emotion.
I felt like I was alive but dead, only yet living to exist.
With great effort, I managed to pull myself up the wall. As I
staggered towards my bathroom, I had to cling to every piece
of furniture that I owned in order not to drop to the floor

again. I knew I didn't have the strength to heave myself up again. Due to the shaking, my knees buckled twice, and I almost fell. I managed to grab hold of something at the last moment and stay on my feet. When I finally leant on the edge of the sink and looked in the mirror, my eyes were blank. My entire skin had lost its colour, it was chalky white. I slowly lifted one hand from the edge of the sink, the person in the mirror did the same thing. I felt like there were hands all over my body. I wanted to shake them off but didn't have the strength. I began to scratch at the places where the phantoms were trying to grab me. My fingernails left furrows in my skin, red lines on a white background. I wanted to stop feeling the way I did right now. I didn't want to be empty anymore. I wanted to finally feel something again, even at the risk of it being pain.

Everything around me started spinning again. My hands that were my only shaky support let go of the sink and I fell backwards to the ground. I didn't even really feel my collision with the stone floor. My head thankfully landed on a stack of washed towels that I didn't have the time to put away earlier.

Soleil

When I saw Jane standing on my doorstep, I knew something wasn't sitting right. Her curly bob was messy, and her Lipstick was smushed over her chin. Black Mascara tears rolled down her cheeks and her body was shaking.
The upper buttons of her blouse had been opened.
"Oh, dear goodness! What happened?", I asked in disbelief.
I made a step into her direction, I wanted to hug her, but within the last second, I made up my mind.
She walked past me like she was in some kind of trance and crashed on my couch. She didn't reek of any alcohol, so what happened?
She sat on my couch, her knees pulled up to her chin, she built up a cage around her. Something terrible must have happened. We had been a couple since forever, but I had never seen her like this. Slowly I came closer to her, bowing down carefully, like she was some kind of scared animal. I saw the disgrace in her eyes, the vivid pain in her iris. Seeing her like this, was one of the worst things I ever lived through.
Was the reason for this maybe also the reason for Janes distant behaviour?
As I came closer to her, I heard her short, heavy breathing. I slowly put out my arm, wanting to softly pet her shoulder, but that probably wasn't the right thing to do.
Whatever happened to her, it seemed to have deeply scarred her. I must not worsen it through any form of wrong behaviour.
"May I?" I asked. My voice so quiet it was barely detectable. I put all the love I felt for her into my eyes, wanting to warm her with myself, trying to warm away the cold in her heart.
Janes head moved up and down, slowly, a gesture so tiny, I wouldn't have grasped it, if I hadn't been looking for it.
I kneeled in front of her, my hand soft and shaky hovering

over her shoulder. I was terrified of doing something wrong, of worsening her situation without wanting to. Her inner restlessness transferred onto me as well. The look in my eyes was serious as I tried to make another step into Janes direction.

"What happened", I asked, my voice soft spoken but urgent. She looked at me, tears uncontrollably running down her face. I wanted to wipe them away so badly, but I knew that I couldn't at this moment. I had to give her all the power, all the control.

When I looked at her suffering face, her eyes of a broken angel, I felt nothing but the need to hold together her shattered world with my bare hands.

When she spoke, her voice was rough, alien "It's Josefine" "What is Josefine?", I asked, around a thousand questions and possible scenarios building up in my head.

I didn't know her, but what happened? Was she sick? Was she alright? Was she-? No, probably not. What happened to this Josefine that threw Jane off like that?

Jane tried to talk, stumbled, stuttered, mumbled, clearly at a loss of words. It took a few minutes until she tried to form her sentence again. "Josefine kissed me. I said no. I did say no. I said I didn't want it, but she just kissed me and touched me" I heard Janes pleading voice, heard the words leaving her mouth, but I was unable to grasp them. What she said took a while to get into my consciousness. My sympathy for Jane broke my heart. How could someone be this heartless, this cruel. I was at the verge of vomiting when I thought about what Jane had to undergo over the course of the last few hours. And I didn't even realize when talking to her on the phone. I blamed myself terribly for not even being alarmed by her behaviour.

I opened my arms for her and this time she nodded, a tiny, faint smile on her lips.

"Thank you for being there", she mumbled. My hand gently

rubbed her arm, and I felt her calming down. "Always! When you are with me, nobody can ever hurt you princess!", I said as quietly. Her head gently laid down in my lap, and as I softly combed through her hair, I felt that she slowly fell asleep.

My head on the other hand was as vivid as ever. In this moment I decided that I would hurt this Josefine. I would revenge my strong, loving, caring girlfriend. *I wanted this bitch to suffer the way Jane suffered because of her.*

Josefine

I woke up in a flash. Had I been asleep? Seemed that way. It was dark outside, my whole body burned, and my head was about to burst. I should most definitely take an Aspirin before going to bed. To be honest, I didn't even really remember how I ended up here. Was this the aftermath of a drunk night out? No, I was quite certain I didn't drink yesterday, and I also didn't leave my apartment.

Then it hit me. All of a sudden, all my memories of the prior evening came back, and I felt like someone had struck me over the head with a wooden panel. I was about to vomit. My limbs were sore and achy. I wasn't able to keep it in any longer. My stomach cramped in a painful manner, and it took all my strength to open the toilet. I felt oddly relieved when yesterday's lunch finally left my stomach. Drenched in sweat I collapsed on the floor again. The taste in my mouth was disgusting. Why for heaven's sake did I react so strongly to a kiss? *A goddam kiss?* It wasn't even my first one, so why was this such a big deal?

I was twenty-three years old, and had multiple relationships during this time, okay one to be fair, but that wasn't important. I most definitely wasn't unkissed and wasn't it normal for friends to experiment?

It wasn't even that odd, as Jane was bi and I was pansexual. So, where was my damned problem? Why was I acting like such a psycho fool? With problems like that, I belonged right in the looney bin. I was a sensitive human being, I knew that. I valued this trait of mine, but it wasn't *that* easy to get me off. I decided that I probably wasn't really over my ex-girlfriend yet, and that this was the reason I acted so strange. Get it together, Josefine! This is not cheating, if you have been separated for multiple years.

I crawled up, using the wall as my help. I flushed the toilet and stumbled into the direction of my bedroom. I was tiered, my brain was fried, and I could have slept whilst standing, but as I laid in bed, it didn't really work.

My eyes were closed, I didn't even have enough energy to open them again, my body was calm, apart from a steady shaking, but my thoughts were out of control.

They revolved all around Jane, not just about what happened today, but around our friendship as a whole.

Our memories were so close, yet so far away, like the stars in the sky. I remembered our shared experiences, but they didn't feel like my own. I felt like I was watching a movie, where I played the protagonist, but I still was just an actress. They were my own memories in a way, but I felt detached from them.

Inside of me, there was only one picture left, clearer than all the other ones before, her lips on mine. This scene burned itself into my retina sending shivers down my spine.

I could feel the exact places where her tongue had touched my mouth. I could make out her warm breath so close to me, that I was able to feel it on my skin. I shrunk, it felt so real for a moment; like she was on top of me again.

Goosebumps appeared in those places, where I still felt her hands on my skin. Ghostlike phantoms refusing to let go of me.

The shivers slowly started to undermine and overtake my whole body. They wandered around my legs, to my knees, my hips, my stomach, reaching my torso, my arms, my neck.

The tendons on my throat began to contract painfully. I opened my eyes, but the only thing I was able to do was staring in the void, my gaze pinned to my bedroom ceiling. My whole body was paralysed, I wasn't able to move, I was trapped.

Over the course of the last few seconds, something must have also happened to my heart, as it was racing indifferently fast and hard. I was scared. Was I about to have a heart attack? My breathing was chaotic and my stomach kept cramping so much that I was terrified I was going to throw up again.

I was staring upwards, my eyes glued to my lamp, a fixing point, giving me the illusion of calmness in the stormy sea of my mind, a sole tear leaving the corner of my eye. Slowly it made its way over my temple, leaving a moist line like a snail, hiding in my hair, as if it was as petrified as me.

I was laying there surviving but dead, unable to move, to make a sound. My existence solely tied to the living corpse in my bed.

It took a heartfelt eternity, but then I noticed my exhaustion slowly sprawling out of the back of my mind again.

I fell into a light and restless sleep.

The ringtone of my alarm painfully transferred me back to reality.

I did sleep, that was clear, but it couldn't have been for long, as my head was pounding and my limbs felt as if they were made of steel.

I felt like there was a tiny person sitting in the back of my head, constantly hammering against my brain, somewhere around the cerebellum and hippocampus.

I slowly got up and tried stretching a little, but I learned that this wasn't too great of an idea. Little black dots started appearing everywhere. My eyesight dimmed, as if there were millions of little insects covering the sun.

I quickly laid back down. I was feeling dizzy; my head was at the verge of bursting. I felt like someone was trying to get my brain through a juicer. Exhaustion paired with pain flashed through my limbs like a lightning bolt.

I needed to breathe… just breathe. In and out and in and out and in…

I slowly tried to lift my body in an upward sitting position resulting in my headache worsening and my sight darkening even more. The pounding in my head had taken over me completely, there was nothing I could do. Game over…

I tried finding something else to focus on. My fingers slowly slid over the cotton of my sheets. I steadily tried to increase the amount of my bodyweight lasting on my legs, while holding on to the corner of my bedframe.

As slow as possible and focused on not putting too great a strain on myself, I tried moving into the direction of my wardrobe.

My fingers were shaking as I carefully tried to push the door open. I usually loved getting up early, just to have this little bit of access time to style myself and feel confident for the day. Well, that was the case *usually*. Today, it already felt draining to solely get out of bed. Half blindly, I reached into my closet and pulled out an oversized sweater and some baggy bottoms. A warm shower would for sure help to take me out of this slump… *at least that was, what I thought.*

I slowly shambled towards my bathroom, trying my best to stay put.

I slowly stripped form my clothes, trying my best not to tremble and trip on something. Falling face down to the floor would be the thing, that would make me seriously question my sanity.

Well, looking back, I would have better tripped and fallen, as questioning my mental health at this point would have been a saint.

I threw my clothes in the direction where I believed my laundry basket to be. While looking up, my gaze accidently brushed over the bathroom mirror. Then, suddenly, something in me clicked.

It felt like gears were starting in my brain, which I didn't know even existed. Out of a weird reflex, I got to my knees to flee from my own frightened embrace.

When I saw myself, only wearing lingerie I suddenly became terrified, but why? Why was I afraid? Nothing regarding my looks had changed over the course of the last few hours. I looked like usual. Maybe the bags under my eyes were a little deeper, a little brighter than usual, but that was it. I really didn't understand what was going on. I never had a problem with seeing myself naked. I actually perceived myself as quite pretty. I used to like my body and the way it looked. But something about that changed. Something about the sight of my undressed self, made me want to vomit.

That was odd. Shaking my head in disbelief, I opened my bra. This wasn't a normal behaviour for a grown woman-

I threw my slip right in the same direction my other clothes went flying in.

But no matter how hard I tried to convince myself that everything was all right, my brain just flat out refused to function normally again.

I carefully prowled inside my shower, watching neatly that I wasn't in sight of any mirroring surfaces.

But as soon I was standing inside of the glass cubicle, it was merely impossible not to get a glance of myself. My shower was built out of glass and stainless steel. Through the glass, I had a perfect view of my bathroom mirror, the stainless steel was an amazing mirror by itself. From every direction, I saw my own scared eyes looking at me. I felt like a frightened deer, surrounded by starving wolves.

I was severely panicking. I didn't know where to look, where it was safe.

I felt like I was at the verge of throwing up again. My gaze agitating trough the room, trying to find just one spot where it was secure for me to place my eyesight.

But it seemed almost impossible to find such a spot, as everything in this damn room seemed to have a shiny surface. It was at this moment, that I started to blame my interior design. It sure looked fabulous, but oh dear was it impractical right now. At least when regarding the circumstances that I was at the verge of turning into a complete psycho maniac. I was turning more and more frail, delicate, weak.

I wasn't even able to make out what I was feeling. Was it shame, was I uncomfortable… no, that wasn't it… But what was it then?

Looking back, I realised how I felt at that moment. I felt dirty. I felt like a second-hand human being. I felt unable to live. I felt like I was stripped from my dignity.

From all this mania, my head started spinning and my circulatory system was dangerously close to collapsing again.

I broke down at the floor of my shower, unable to do anything, unable to move, to breathe, only my thoughts were going absolutely bonkers.

My whole body was shaking. What was going on? What was wrong with me? Was I able to be *not* weird for once? Was being normal *really* not an option? God dammit?! Even though I couldn't really do something about my situation as I had no idea how it emerged, I was starting to get angry at myself.

I got up defiantly, ignoring my dizziness and the fact that the pain in my head was about to knock me out.

What was wrong about the thought of passing out? I deserved it. I was going completely crackers, so passing out was exactly what I deserved. I deserved it. I so damn deserved it. Why couldn't I be normal? Why couldn't I be a normal, functioning human being? Why did I always had to dramatize everything so profoundly?

Due to recent evets, I decided not to shower that morning. After using some dry shampoo on my hair, I reached for my make-up back that was resting on the counter.

I looked myself in the eye, my gaze fixated on the mirror. I slowly put down the bag again, as I honestly didn't have enough energy to get myself ready as usual. Even the bare minimum seemed unarchivable, so any extras were merely impossible.

Also, why would I wear makeup? I didn't deserve make up. I was human trash and fooling everybody into believing that I wasn't would have been a blunt lie.

Even though I wasn't hungry at all, I made myself eat an apple before leaving the house.

The stinging in my stomach was unbearable but after two and a half doses of paracetamol it decreased to a level that made walking a torture, but possible.

My first class for today was German language studies together with Jane. As I entered the auditorium ten minutes early- as usual, I saw Jane already waving into my direction. A part of me had wished that she wouldn't be there, but these thoughts were diminished now. My stomach began cramping up again, but I brushed it of as hunger because I didn't have a proper breakfast.

I forced a smile upon my lips and sat beside my best friend. "You look terrible. What is going on?", Jane asked, as soon as I put down my bag. "Had bad dreams" I mumbled.

Everything was normal between us, no mention of our kiss or our meeting yesterday, so I decided not to talk about it as well. I knew it! It was just something you do with your friends. Nothing out of the ordinary, not even worth a mention. Nothing bad had happened and I had just been too clueless to understand these social cues.

Jane was the first friend I ever had. She meant the world to me, and I knew that she would never do anything to hurt me. But the absurd feeling stayed. What was up with me today? The day went on as slow as if time was running backwards. And when I got home that evening, I was unusually tiered. It was only 7pm, and I normally worked late nights. Well, then again I had been really busy today. I had… Wait- I hadn't really done that much. I actually worked *less* than usual. I didn't do anything even worth the mention, but my brain felt like someone stamped on it and my body was aching as if I had done eight hours of heigh performance sports. I decided to shower tonight as I wanted to prevent another disaster in the morning. I also couldn't and wouldn't go another day with dry shampoo. I already had felt disgusting today. I wouldn't do this two days in a row- definitely not!

Hoping that this might help, I opened my closet drawer and took out a bikini. Afterwards I took off all my clothes with my eyes closed- which I can tell you is harder to accomplish then one might figure. By the time I finally managed to put my swimwear on, I must have tripped over around a thousand times.

When I opened my eyes, I was standing right in front of a mirror- my newest arch enemy. I looked at my reflection, my reflection looked back at me, fixating my body with its gaze. Even though the most crucial parts of me were covered, I felt my stomach beginning to twist again. I felt like there was a small metal ball inside of me, growing steadily by the minute. I took a deep breath, trying my best to properly calm myself down. If I just breathed right, I would be able to trigger my parasympathetic nervous system. Logic and rationalism always helped me to calm down, but at that moment, it didn't really seem to work.

I felt my uterus painfully cramping up and suddenly, there were Janes hands all over me again.

These phantom hands burned themselves into me like blazing fire, penetrating my skin so long until I could feel their branding on my bones.

It took every bit of strength in me to leave my bedroom and move into the direction of my bathroom. My body knew what was about to come, and with every slow step, my fate became less reversable. When I finally entered, I bend down, crawling over the floor until I reached the window. Even though it was a non-see-through glass I felt like somebody was watching me. I pulled down the blinders and switched on the small lamp over the bathroom mirror. I tried to shun the big ceiling light, so I wouldn't be able to see my reflection properly, just silhouettes.

The absence of light could have been romantic under different circumstances, but now, it just helped me get my way. I felt unclean and disgusting. I needed to get rid of the dry shampoo in my hair. I only realised that my knees where shaking as I made a few tiny, timid steps towards the shower.

I was covered in goosebumps. I was hot and cold at the same time. Why was taking a shower so hard for me out of the blue?

Surprisingly this realization didn't make my blood boil the way it did just this morning. When I listened to my intuition, I knew that anger wasn't going to help eighter way.

I slowly crossed my arms in front of my chest, my torso, my waist. I could feel the goosebumps getting more intense. My fingernails dug into the skin over my ribcage, leaving red marks on my pale flesh. I hugged myself so tightly, it felt like I was suffocating me, nearly crushing my bones.

When my hands loosened up, slowly letting me go, there were deep red carvings in my skin, notches, where my fingernails had tried to show their love so desperately that they created an irreversible monument of suffrage.

My arms kept on being crossed in front of my chest, my ribs clearly showing through my skin.

I sat in the shower cabin fully made of glass and metal. My gaze was intentionally fixated forward, solicitous not to get the door hinge in eyesight.

Blindly, I longed for the showerhead. When the water started running, I shrugged. Damn it, cold!

My hand moved the thermostat carefully to the right.

Warmth! I usually enjoyed letting myself be taken in by the warm water running down my body, heating up not only my body but also my soul. Usually, I used a hot shower as a method for lighting my mood. Today, I only showered for the sake of cleaning myself. Today, the water only warmed me from the outside, leaving this icy cold, numb feeling inside of my heart, refusing to wash it down.

I still tried to let the water wrap around me like a blanket, shielding me from my dark thoughts. This worked surprisingly well as my abdominal pain wandered in the back of my head for the first time today.

Even though it wasn't the feeling of soothing secrecy, I still felt better. The water cleaned me from everything, from every dark little thought-monster, from all the pain inside of me, from everything.

With my eyes closed, I fumbled for the shampoo bottle and poured a little of its contents into the palm of my hand. Slowly, I began to lather my blonde hair. The foam ran down my face, something that usually bothered me tremendously, but today I simply didn't care. I hardly noticed it. Slowly, the soap washed off my head. I realised how the water was slowly washing my hair from the lather at the back of my head onto my shoulders. I felt the tickling sensation of the ends intensely on my bare skin. I breathed through my mouth, deeply... in and out, over and over, in and out.

When I finally opened my eyes, it almost hit me.

I was surrounded by a hazy fog that was so thick I could barely breathe through my nose. I could only vaguely recognise everything around me. I quite literally perceived my world as if through a clouded veil. When I finally managed to decipher the numbers on my wall clock, there was no need to ask myself where this immense amount of humidity was coming from.

I had been sitting there for forty minutes without even realising it, without thinking, without being a part of this reality.

My eyes closed, my emotions switched off, unable to form a clear thought and- to all appearances, completely without a sense of time. I stood up slowly, apathetically staring at one spot so as not to get a reflection of myself anywhere in my field of vision.

My blood pressure skyrocketed, clearly, I could have guessed, but I had not uttered a thought into that direction. The blood was pounding in my eye sockets and in the part of my brain where I estimated the hippocampus and thalamus to be. I felt dizzier than ever. Small, but then rapidly increasing spots formed on the surface of my vision. After just half a minute, I could see almost nothing apart from an agitated black colour. This reaction was quite logical, considering that I had just sat there for so long in such a humid heat. I propped myself up against the wall, breathing heavily, almost wheezing. I groped for a towel. My fingers found one and clutched it. I wrapped it around my body, felt the fabric against my skin and made sure that my hair as well disappeared under a towel. I just stood there motionless for a few minutes, waiting for my vision to clear and my dizziness to gradually subside. Then I opened a drawer, took out a microfibre cloth and used it to wipe the fogged-up mirror. Mistake! A serious mistake, as it turned out. My gaze lingered on me, on my reflection, my eyes locked in on themselves, pure terror written inside of them.

I paused mid-motion. My hands weakened and my grip on the cloth loosened which caused it to slip from my grasp, landing in the sink, where it remained and slowly darkened in colour, absorbing all the liquid. My hand slowly and weakly sank onto the shelf under the mirror on which the washbasin was mounted. My shoulders, my neck, my legs, my arms, my back, even my feet suddenly contracted, only to relax again in a flash. It was as if I had been hit by an electric bolt, no more

27

than a few seconds though. I staggered back a few steps and dropped onto the closed toilet lid wrapped in just my towel. I simply sat there, not knowing what was wrong with me. My thoughts were like a rollercoaster, going round and round in circles, making smaller and smaller turns until they finally faded away almost completely. I thought nothing, or did I think everything at once? In any case, no matter how hard I tried, I no longer managed to grasp one thought. I didn't even know exactly what I was feeling... Pain? Anger? Despair? Or maybe sadness, freedom? Freedom that was so profound that it dragged me into the abyss?

I stared straight ahead, my gaze acquiring an apathetic emptiness. As if someone had flipped a switch, all this emotional chaos suddenly disappeared. It was replaced by a yawning emptiness. I sat there, stiff and tense. The emptiness set in like a wave that pushed everything inside of me out of the way. I could almost feel it physically, because I felt nothing at all.

My insides felt cleansed, but not in that pleasant and redemptive way, more like a computer that had its software hijacked. It just felt terrible. I wanted to cry; just let it all pour out of me because I knew I was in a terrible place. My mind told me so, but my body contradicted it, putting emptiness where there had just been absolute hullabaloo. I wanted to scream as loud as I could, but I remained silent because my body was numb, trying to make me believe that there was nothing worth screaming about. I no longer had the control over my body, my brain was receiving my signals, but it wasn't responding. It just didn't want to do what I told it to.

I continued to stare at the counter with a look as blank as that of a dead woman, noticing my cosmetics bag at the edge. My gaze wandered without me telling it to, wandered further and got stuck.

I was now at a point where, for better or worse, I had to accept that I had completely lost control over my body. I was no longer thinking, just doing what my body told me to. I had lost my power, my body no longer did what I said, my brain comprehended what my body demanded. My gaze wandered until it finally caught on something, a greyish silver-coloured case made of sturdy fabric and black stitching. My hand reached out for it and my fingers opened the shiny magnetic clasp. I didn't feel it. I realised I was doing it but the touch of my fingertips on the fabric and metal didn't penetrate my consciousness. I was numb, emotionally blind.

I opened the case, a set: tweezers, nail file, scissors. It was the last that I clumsily removed from the small case before dropping the rest back on the shelf. I turned the shiny stainless steel in my hand, between my fingers. I saw how my skin was pressed down where the two closed edges came together in one spot. I knew it was supposed to tug, but it didn't.

I let the tip of the scissors run gently over my skin, watching, watching the little white lines it left on my red skin.
It was like watching the white streaks left by aeroplanes as they glided across the sky as a child. I couldn't really describe it, but at that moment something magical emanated from those scissors. It was as if they were shouting at me "I am the solution to all your problems! I am what you need. Here! Me! I'm the key", and at the same time they were begging for some attention, for someone to finally take care of them for once. There I was, holding the metal thing in my hand, giving it attention, the attention it had been asking for, the attention that no one was giving to me. It was healing to give someone else what I so desperately needed myself. I did what one does with scissors, opened them, closed them, opened them, closed them, opened them. Snip. Snap. Snip. Snap. Snip.
And with every time I did it, the screaming, the desire became louder "Use me! Appreciate me! I just want to be used." I

pulled my fingers out of the eyelets and gripped the open scissors by their hinge. My phalanges were shaky as I began to apply a little more pressure on my skin. The white lines I was leaving on myself became clearer, more visible, more intense. It made me feel powerful and free to do what I did. The reason for this feeling was intangible, it was in the air, but it was impossible to capture. One could compare it to desperately trying to grab a scent out of the air with your bare hands and put it into a jar. *It does not work.* I continued my circles. It wasn't voluntary, but it gave me the illusion of freedom. I didn't feel it, yet it gave me the delusion of power. My movements became tighter and tighter, and the circles the blade drew became smaller and smaller. Eventually, the blade stopped motionless at a point on my left hand, just above the joint of my thumb. I realised... the foreplay was over now.

It was time for me to submit powerlessly to myself, or whoever it was that was controlling me.

I realised the blade in my skin before I realised that I was the one wielding it. I started moving and could hear the tip of the scissors cutting through the top layer of my skin, meeting resistance again and again. Once about a centimetre had been overcome, I lifted the blade from my skin, returned it to the starting point and the procedure was repeated, again and again, and each time there was less resistance.
My skin bowed to its fate, just as I bowed to my own.
After repeating this process a few times, I noticed blood beginning to ooze from the wound. The cut turned red from the centre, the colour moved further and further outwards until it reached the end. My eyes rested on the gash. I saw the welt on my skin without realising that it truly existed. It was surreal to me, I could see it, grasp it with my eyes, but I couldn't feel it. There was only a tingling sensation in my hand, no pain where it was supposed to be - surreal! I can feel everything

that is part of me, a basic human principle that could not simply be thrown out of joint. No! That could not... That could not be reality. I noticed tears welling up in my eyes, I was so overwhelmed, I felt so small, so lonely, so helpless, but *I felt*. I realised that I was feeling again that I seemed to have broken through the wall of emptiness, but now the dam broke and the emotions engulfed me in grotesque waves. I felt happy to feel, felt helpless because I didn't know what was happening to me, and more importantly why. I felt distraught because I didn't know how to help myself, I couldn't get out of this loop of misery that I didn't even know how I had gotten into. It was as if someone had simply flicked a switch and made a decision about my life without asking for my consent first.

I stood up, feeling like a robot that did everything it was told to do on command, feeling programmed, because there was no other way to explain the almost routine movements with which I now washed off the blood and stuck a band-aid over my cut. I covered up all traces. I had to make sure that no residue- however small, remained from what had just happened. It was like trying to cover up a murder, only that I was the perpetrator, victim and investigator all at the same time. I felt the need to hide the part of me that had just revealed itself away from the rest of me. It was as if my psyche was vehemently refusing to reveal to me what had been wrong with it for the last two days. I was exhausted, not just physically, but mentally as well. I felt like I could fall asleep in the very spot I was in. I pulled myself to my feet and was surprised to suddenly find myself in an absolute elation. I got dressed, blow-dried my hair, brushed my teeth, overcome by a sudden energy as if I had just woken up from a three-day comatose sleep. I hummed a song. I let 'Ghost Town' by Benson Boone fill my entire head. 'Maybe loving me's the reason you can't love

yourself. Before I turn your heart into a ghost town, show me everything we've built so I can tear it all down'
I loved these lines. I loved them because I found them profound and beautiful, empathetic, but right now they were only a means to an end. I had to manage maintaining the energy that had just appeared, frantically. I sang, I hummed, I lost myself in music. Anything to avoid having to think. Anything to avoid having to ask myself the question; what had just happened here? And even more so; why?

What was wrong with me?

And there they were again, the thought shadows that laid over me like a thundercloud. Checkmate. Hit, sunk.
I couldn't escape myself after all... unfortunately. I was trapped in my own skin. In my skin that no longer seemed to belong to me. *My wounded, cut skin.*
With the realisation that my problems didn't seem to have vanished into thin air after all, my tiredness suddenly returned. I only slept for an hour that night and it wasn't even in one piece.
As soon as I got some rest, my thoughts, my questions, the indefinable images in my head caught up to me again.
I tossed and turned, dozed off, woke up again, cried, rolled over, dozed off again, only to wake up a few minutes later, drenched in sweat and terrified.

Restlessness. My thoughts were restless.

When my alarm clock rang the next morning, I was dead tired. I couldn't go on like this, I told myself. I made the decision to finally return to normality. My head really had been going crazy for long enough. I had to function. Studying didn't just happen by itself, and the chores had to be done as well.

Jane

When Josefine entered the lecture hall, I couldn't believe my eyes because there was a wide smile on her lips. It was a Josefine smile, only she could light up a whole room when she lifted the corners of her mouth. This was the girl I had befriended ages ago and had recently fallen in love with. However, I was surprised to see that same smile playing on her lips this morning. Yesterday she had seemed so distant, completely absent and not at all focused. I hadn't the faintest idea why she suddenly seemed to be her old self again. Yesterday I had feared that she had *actually understood* what had happened between us.

I was confused, and to all appearances, this was also evident on my face, because when Josefine stood in front of me, she tilted her head and furrowed her brow. "Earth to Jane! Heeeellooooo? Anyone home?"

I quickly tried to regain my composure.

Everything was as usual. Our friendship seemed to be intact. Our friendship... How I loathed these circumstances. I didn't just want to be her friend. I wanted more. I wanted to pull her close, kiss her, taste her again. No matter the cost...

But maybe it didn't have to come to that.

Maybe... Maybe Josefine's sudden change of mood was because she had realised that she reciprocated my feelings, that she loved me too.

Josefine

Looking Jane in the eye again and behaving as if everything was completely normal was strange. I still felt this unquenchable nausea in my stomach that wouldn't go away even when I dropped into the seat next to her. I still didn't realise why I had become so self-conscious about being in her presence. I still didn't understand why I had recently become so sensitive to Jane's company, but I realised that I had to stop, otherwise I would be ruining our friendship. Nothing could be as important as the connection I had with Jane. We had known each other forever and I loved her with all my heart. She was sacred to me.

How could I ever jeopardise something so fundamentally important?

My head would calm down eventually, and until then it was easy for me to just pretend that everything was fine.

I would just keep convincing everyone else until I was convinced myself.

That's how I got through the day. I attended my two lectures, chatted to a handful of comrades with Jane and laughed. I laughed, and laughed, and laughed. Laughter was my trademark. I was the one who brought good humour wherever I went. It was just a shame that it was only partly sincere today. My stomachache was eating away at me and a headache set in around midday. Great!

I defiantly pulled a packet of paracetamol out of my bag and swallowed two of the tablets before rejoining the group.

But it just didn't get any better. On the contrary... The longer I sat in the café with Jane and the others, sipping my vanilla chai latte, the worse it got. When I eventually started to see black spots again, I got up and said goodbye. Harper held me by the arm.

"You want to go already?" she asked with a feigned sadness. "Why don't you stay just a little longer?"

"Sorry... I've just got so much to do" I replied. "I still have to finish a term paper by Monday." I couldn't think of a better excuse. "In which subject?" Harper couldn't be shaken off.

"German studies"

"Oh god... I've already heard. Your professor is supposed to be pure hell."

I nodded. "Totally. Well, see you in a few days!"

I felt terrible. Not only because the pain almost made me collapse, but also because I had just lied to one of my closest friends.

What had become of me?

When I got home, I threw myself onto the couch and decided to simply distract myself from reality. I picked up my mobile phone and tapped on the gallery icon. My internal storage had been complaining that it had too little capacity left for ages. Time to take care of this matter.

I scrolled down, slowly and carefully, to find images that I could delete, but soon my mind began to wander. That picture, yes... I had been in Vienna, at the Prata, and there. There I was, grinning broadly into the camera with Jane. Unbelievable...

And then, I stumbled across a portrait of myself that I hadn't seen in an eternity. It was a simple pencil drawing in an almost manga style, showing a character that looked almost exactly like me. I liked this picture. It combined art with a slight flair of exuberance. Out of intuition, I opened WhatsApp and clicked on the settings. I then uploaded this drawing as my new profile picture. It made me smile. It was a real smile, and it felt good.

I closed my eyes; I was exhausted. I deleted all the open tabs on my mobile phone before putting it on standby and laying it on my stomach. My head rested lightly on the armrest of my

couch and my eyes closed again. This time I let it happen.
But apparently, I wasn't granted a longer period of peace, as it didn't take five minutes before I was jolted out of my thoughts by the ringtone I had set for important messages.

Groaning, I sat up, only to turn around and lie on my stomach with my mobile phone in my hand.

A message from Jane.

"Who drew your profile picture?" Followed by a smugly smiling emoji and one with a kissy face.

"Don't know" I wrote, which was true. The drawing was a screenshot taken from my father's Facebook account.

I realised how dismissive my message must have sounded, so I put a "What do you think?" after it.

I didn't have to wait a minute before I could see Jane's reply on my display, and it made everything in my stomach start to tighten painfully again.

"Looks hot" these emojis again, this time followed by a tearful, laughing face. Something like that shouldn't upset me too much. That was Jane's humour. Not a day of our friendship had gone by without her making a dirty joke. I appreciated that about her. She was self-confident, and she made such jokes in a way that they weren't off-putting, but simply poignantly funny. I just didn't know what my head had been trying to boycott recently. I couldn't explain my behaviour...

I also replied with a laughing emoji and the obligatory red heart that was part of our chat history at all times.

I hoped I had defused the situation... *wait, there was nothing to defuse.* I was just acting crazy beyond all reason, that was all. But Jane seemed to be in a particularly good mood today, because she followed up with "Looks hot, like you!" By now I wasn't even wondering about the attached faces that Jane seemed to think were so humorous. The emojis I sent back in response were dripping with overwhelm and friendly distance, but then I changed my mind. Jane and I were friends. This was nothing but a funny joke. I had to react normally. I put a "You too" with the smiley faces Jane had chosen behind it.

I immediately got a reply. "Really?!" followed by a "Thank you". Again, with that horrible emoji that I wouldn't even use if I was seriously flirting with someone.

I responded with a casual "yes" to Jane's question, because it was true. I thought all my friends were beautiful and I could understand anyone wanting to date them, except that I just loved them all in a platonic manner.

When I looked at my screen again to read Jane's new message, I had to shake my head.

Today it was really impossible to get rid of her.

"What can this mean..." was written there. Again, the emoji. Mentally, I rolled my eyes a little. I was tired. I didn't feel like being flirted with any longer.

"Nothing" I typed into my text field, but realised at the last moment before I pressed the send button that this sounded rather belligerent and unnecessarily harsh, so I added a laughing emoji.

As was to be expected, the reply read resigned. I knew that most of it was just feigned grief and the rest of it was because I didn't feel like messing around any more.

"Oh that's a shame..." Along with an exaggeratedly depressed-looking emoji and a kissy face.

I made up my mind. She hadn't done anything to me, and it really wasn't her fault that I was about to fall asleep.

"I didn't mean it like that... in a friendly way, of course" I texted, and even added the smugly smiling emoji for her sake. Even before I could read Jane's reply, I realised that I had just started a new round of her little game. And of course it was exactly that way... I just knew her too well.

"Come over..." was the message that had just appeared on my

display. A mixture of laughter and groans came out of my mouth. I had brought it upon myself. Oh well...

I was starting to get fed up and I really felt like I was potentially giving Jane the wrong idea. I sent a laughing smiley face and a shrugging emoji in response.

When she only replied with a kissy face, I thought I had finally achieved my goal and first closed the app and then my eyes.

Or so I thought...

Less than a minute later, Jane's next message arrived in the form of a beep on my phone. Argg...

My desire to simply not open the message and pretend I hadn't seen it continued to grow, but I did manage to check my lock screen to see what else Jane had to say. It might be something important...

But what I read now left me confused because I couldn't make sense of it.

The words "It wasn't" lit up on my screen. Context?

My curiosity got the better of me and I unlocked my mobile phone to open our chat. Yes, I hadn't misread it. "It wasn't" that's what the text said. Without emojis, unusually serious for Jane. She had referred to my message again, the one in which I had said that everything was supposed to be platonic on my part, of course. "It wasn't." now that I had some sort of context, I knew even less what Jane was asking me.

Did she think I saw her as more than just a friend?

Was this her way of confronting me? I didn't know how to respond to "It wasn't", so I just sent her back a question mark. Suddenly there was no sign of the fatigue that had just threatened to engulf me. Did Jane seriously think I was just playing games with her? Did she really think my feelings were secretly different to the ones I openly admitted?

Or did she like...

Jane's reply abruptly interrupted my merry-go-round of thoughts. "Not from my side" That tension again, that serious-ness due to the missing little smiley faces. How I wished I could go back to just now, when Jane was clearly joking. Now, I could no longer tell. She liked to be sarcastic at times and teased me about the fact that I often didn't realise when she was pulling my leg again, especially not via text messages. "Really?" I asked.

"You look really hot" came back from Jane, and, as if to make it even clearer, she replied to the message with my question with "Yes".

At first, I was confused, maybe a little shocked, but in any case I felt very uncomfortable. Jane was regularly a little bit over the top, but one could usually tell when she was joking. Right now, it wasn't the joking Jane I was talking to, and that con-cerned me. I felt that I was texting with the Jane who meant everything she said, but I quickly pushed that thought to the back of my mind. That couldn't be true... No, that was just Jane's nature. She was just testing out a new kind of humour on me in a perfidious way.

I needed clarity, that was obvious from my answer. Jane would now resolve that she had only made a joke. We would laugh and we would talk about something else.

"What do you mean, I can't hear your voice, and I don't want there to be any misunderstandings" I added an emoji with a heart to let Jane know that she shouldn't take my message in any way maliciously.

"I like girls as much as I like boys"

I didn't understand. No, actually I did understand. I had actu-ally understood the direction this conversation was taking for a long time, but I just didn't want to accept it. My friendship with Jane meant so much to me, I couldn't let her drive it against the wall and destroy it like that.

I played dumb. I had to give her the chance to row back as

often as possible, but unfortunately, I was already aware of how incredibly low my chances of success were.

When Jane set her mind to something, she went through with whatever she set her mind to. That was just the way she was, and usually this determination was one of the qualities that made me appreciate her so much. Only now it was clearly becoming a burden.

"Me too" I texted back. Quite neutrally. A fact that she already knew, without any reference to Jane's hints. Along the lines of: So, what's the news? Unfortunately, I already knew what the news was.

No. Wrong. I didn't actually *know*. I only suspected it, and maybe I was doing Jane completely dirty. Maybe she had just realised that I hadn't been doing so well over the course of the last few days, and she wanted to be nice to me. Yes, that had to be it!

And then there was Jane's reply.

"I think you're incredibly gorgeous"

Gorgeous. It had been clear that she would overlook the hint I'd given her. Here we went again, so I wrote. "But you mean it in a friendly way..."

I didn't really care how obtuse she must have thought I was, the main thing was that she finally realised that this conversation had fallen into a niche that I didn't feel at all comfortable in and that I wanted to get out of as quickly as possible.

"The kiss was great"

The kiss, that goddamn kiss. I hadn't really been in favour of it from the start. My goodness, as if my gut had already predicted something like that.

I was no longer just overwhelmed; I was panicking. I was in a quandary. I loved Jane more than anything, wanted to give her the world, wanted to please her. I wanted her to be happy and if there was one thing I absolutely did not want, it was to hurt her.

"Yes" I wrote, more to buy time than to agree with her, but thankfully she didn't take it that way either.

"At least for me" I read from her.

Very well. "Not so much for me" I typed into the text field. I stared at the message. I stared at the black paper aeroplane symbol on the green background and still didn't have the courage to send the message. I knew that what I was about to do was wrong, but I couldn't help it. I knew how strongly Jane felt emotions. I knew she wouldn't be able to handle my response. I erased the words and instead wrote; "There was something about it..." It was true, there was something about it... something horrible, something not exactly disgusting, but something that just felt *wrong*. She was like a sister to me... it was as if a sister had kissed me.

Besides, Jane knew me. If she was reading this message, she knew I didn't sound like that when I was serious. I didn't usually text like that. My message didn't sound authentic, it sounded forced. My message sounded the way waiters looked when they had to be polite to a customer who had reordered their food three times and then 'patronisingly' tipped three cents. Forced. Forcefully.

But apparently Jane didn't want to hear that I loved her in a platonic way any more than I wanted to hear that she didn't.

"I agree" was Jane's latest message, only she meant it differently.

I decided to return to the complete truth, *my* complete truth. Well, maybe to a sugar-coated version of it. "I was a little overwhelmed by the situation" I wrote. That was such an understatement that it could almost pass as a stylistic device, but it was true.

"I know" she wrote. Wait, what?

She knew? How?

Some things just couldn't be handled via chat, so I typed:

"Wait a minute. I'll call you"

I realised that at this point it was a foregone conclusion that Jane was going to tell me exactly what she wanted to tell me. I couldn't escape any longer. What was I supposed to do? I didn't want to hurt her, never. No matter what the cost. And maybe if I was in a relationship with her, maybe...

No, that wasn't an option. I felt nothing for her in that way and I had to find a gentle but firm approach to make that clear to her. I had to assert myself, I...

But I was also not under any circumstances allowed to hurt Jane.

My finger trembled over the telephone symbol. I wasn't ready to call. I couldn't face up to it yet, but I had to. Whether I was ready or not. Jane had decided today was the right time to tell me that her feelings for me were beyond platonic measures, and now it was up to me to find a solution. After all, it was my fault that her bobble would burst. I would inevitably hurt her. I would be the bad guy in the situation and there was no real way out for me. Except...

I took a deep breath, closed my eyes and clicked on the call icon to start a video chat. I needed to see Jane's face. I could no longer have such a serious conversation with the screen of my mobile phone.

Before she had a chance to take the call, I sat up straight and fixed my hair. I didn't want to look how I felt... miserable. A dial tone buzzed, and Jane's face appeared pixelated on my screen. "Hey" I said. It sounded cautious, restrained.

"Hi" Jane didn't seem as confident as usual either.

"German studies term paper, then..." She grinned. "That's interesting, why don't I know anything about it when we sit next to each other in every seminar?" I looked at Jane, caught off guard. I couldn't lie, I had never been able to, to be precise.

"Yeah, well" I nodded. "You've got me there. I wasn't feeling well, and I didn't feel like arguing. I wanted to go home"

"I don't believe you" Jane replied with a sudden seriousness in her voice that drove my nausea to a zenith.

"What do you mean?" my voice was trembling. I hadn't said anything wrong...

"Josefine, you're avoiding me. You're not feeling ill. You don't want to see me anymore"

"No, of course not!" How could she think that? "I would never avoid you. I love spending time with you." She laughed. "Of course" Why was her tone suddenly so sarcastic? And why did I think to recognised a hint of contempt in it?

"Jane, what's going on? Wasn't everything okay just now? Of course I like spending time with you. I love you! You're my best friend..." That laugh again.

"Josefine, if you lie once, you won't be trusted ever again", this time her disapproval was clearly perceptible. I wasn't imagining the whole thing.

"Jane" I exhaled noisily. "You misunderstood me. No, God... of course it's not your fault. I misspoke"

She raised an eyebrow.

"I would never lie to you, but you know how Harper is. I just didn't have the strength today to explain to her at length why I wanted to leave. Okay? It really, really, really had nothing to do with you!"

I panicked. Could Jane really have misunderstood me like that? I loved her so much and I told her so every day. How could she have forgotten? I felt like a terrible friend. And rightly so. I was, after all. Maybe not directly towards Jane, but definitely towards Harper. And I had hurt Jane as well. I didn't deserve either one of them.

They were always so good to me, and then I ended up treating them like that. I should be ashamed of myself. And I was. Nevertheless, I profoundly was. "I'm really sorry Jane" she nodded slightly "I really am. I don't know how I deserve you." "With behaviour like that, certainly not" she said, before her features softened again and she looked at me. Now with this soft, meaningful look in her eyes that I couldn't interpret. Where had this sudden change of heart come from? I couldn't explain it for the life of me until... until Jane opened her mouth and continued speaking. Now came the part I had been dreading. Now came the part where I would have to be an even worse friend, because I would have to answer honestly. I was a terrible, terrible person.

"Josefine... I forgive you, because I think you're incredibly amazing" she paused briefly, only to continue straight away. No, she shouldn't go on. She shouldn't ruin everything we had. "Our kiss... I didn't just think it was objectively good. I've never felt anything like it. It was incredible... As incredible as you"

Oh.my.god! She was really going to do it.
"I think I've fallen in love with you, Josefine"
And it was out. She had said it; I had heard it. It was irreversible. I had to answer. Goodness, how tempting the red phone button seemed. But no, I had to face up the situation.
I took a deep breath. "Jane, listen to me. I really love you..." I was such a bad friend.
"...but only in a platonic way. Please don't get me wrong, I think you're wonderful, but I'm not in love with you" I saw the enthusiastic gleam slowly disappear from her eyes.
"Oh Jane... I just don't want to lose what we already have. Our friendship is so meaningful to me, imagine if we didn't end up together and then all this would be ruined as well."
She sighed, but still didn't say anything.
I looked at her. "Why don't you say something?"
"You know Lil, that's what I meant. You're a horrible friend"
Her answer hit me like a punch in the gut. She called me Lil, after my middle name, as she had been doing for a year. It

was her special nickname for me. "I'm truly terribly sorry! I wish I could reciprocate your feelings. Please tell me what I can do better. I wish with all my heart I could be a better friend to you!" She took a breath.

"That's not the point here, Josefine. I want you to see what an opportunity this would be for you. Imagine what a couple we would be. Please... give us a chance. If you really want to do something good for me, then give us a chance, will you? We can still be friends if it doesn't work out"

"Jane, but I don't love you in that way" I wanted to say, but I didn't. I was a lousy friend, that's what she had said. I wish I could - wait, I could. She had given me the chance to make up for my terrible behaviour towards her. I didn't reciprocate her feelings... *yet.*

Who said it had to stay that way. Objectively speaking, she was very pretty. Her dark curls, her hazel eyes, her beautiful features. Yes, objectively I had probably won the jackpot, I should consider myself lucky.

On the other hand... she had been one of my closest friends for years and I had never wasted a single thought on wanting more of her-

Stop! That wasn't the point here. Just because Jane had once again drawn better conclusions than me. She was right, we would definitely be a wonderful fit for each other. Would we? We-

Besides, this was my chance to prove to her that I was a worthy friend, that I was deserving of her love. I decided to give in. No, giving in sounded so negative, so much like manipulation... That was nonsense. Jane would never do anything like that. She was the personification of an angel. She was wonderful. I decided to give it a chance... yes, that sounded better.

"Very well..." I said. "Let's give it a go" "Really?" Jane looked genuinely surprised. She seemed pleased, it seemed to be working. I was a good friend. *I was a good friend.* I was a good

45

friend! My heart felt relieved, but my stomach decided to speak up for itself. I felt sick.

It was worth it though. Jane was worth it. Besides, there was no connection between Jane and my pain. It wasn't as if Jane was poisoning my food or anything like that. No, Jane was just there, and my body was going crazy. Maybe I really was in love with her after all. Didn't they say that people in love even felt their attraction physically? And my stomach pains were - yes, since when had they actually occurred? That's right. Ever since Jane had taken the initiative to kiss me.
She had been right, yes, she had realised it. How could I have said no?
Ever since Jane had kissed me, my body seemed to be painfully trying to tell me that we belonged together. It had to be that way...
"Yes" I replied. I nodded.
When I saw Jane's broad grin, I had to smile as well. I made it. I had made Jane happy. *I would finally have the chance to prove myself worthy of her love.*
All of a sudden, Jane looked serious again. She looked at me and said: "You know, I always seem so confident"
She paused. There was a certain kind of calculating shyness in her gaze.
"Yes?" I asked cautiously. "You can tell me anything Jane. You know me, I would never judge you"
She breathed and continued to look at me guardedly.
"No... I can't say that. I can't ask you to do that"
"Jane...why don't you talk to me? It's okay. I don't bite"
Her expression changed to a grin as she said "You're welcome to bite me anytime"
I didn't comment on that suggestion as her face immediately became serious again.
"Lil, I don't want you to think that I don't have our backs..."

Us... that sounded weird, and it made me feel uncomfortable. Probably only because it was new. Yes, it had to be that way. New things scared me- apparently, and this was the perfect kind of exposure therapy. "...because I'm entirely and completely invested in our relationship, but..."

Relationship... there really was a lot that I- or rather my stomach, had to get used to.

"...what I'm saying is that I'd like our relationship to remain a secret for a little while. I'm sure you're the one I'm in love with..."

Fine, well, she was apparently the only one of us- no, that sounded mean. I loved her too, my body had been frantically trying to tell me that over the last few days, but was that really it?

"So please don't get me wrong, I love you more than anything, but I just think we should grow close to each other in private before we make it official so that nothing can shake us apart"

I had no objections. "I realise that this must sound hypocritical, but I'm just afraid that someone around us might react homophobically..."

Jane

I really nailed it... the homophobia ploy. I knew that it would strike a chord with Josefine. After all, I had seen the comments under her last CSD post. "Burn that disgusting flag", "People like you, that should be illegal"

Of course I was annoyed to read something like that, as it was also directed at me and Soleil, who I had been head over heels in love with at the time, but I realised how useful it was for me at this moment. Now, things were different with Soleil as well. I no longer loved her. Sure, she was friendly and caring, but she just wasn't my cup of tea anymore. I got bored of her after a while. I knew that beforehand, but I didn't care at the time. I was quite intelligent, but I had been in love. And as is the case with love, you do things that you wouldn't do under any other circumstances. You no longer acted rationally. You might still think, but you no longer acted upon these thoughts, but purely on your love for the other person.

It was just darn impractical because I now had her stuck to me for the rest of my university career. I didn't really care about her anymore. If it was up to me, I would have broken up with her ages ago, but unfortunately things couldn't go my way if I cherished my degree. Soleil's father was my political science professor, and unfortunately, I knew all too well how much he loved and protected his daughter. When we first met over dinner, we didn't get off to a very good start, as he had no doubt assumed I was a man. I had also realised this from the marks under my term papers. But I didn't care about that.

For Soleil's sake, I had improved my relationship with her father and- as a result, my grades did as well.

Now however, I was under the premises that I couldn't break up with Soleil under any circumstances. Nevertheless, I had to get together with Josefine. She was my life. I just couldn't bear to be without her any longer. She had to be mine. I had made sure of that. I knew her inside and out. I knew exactly which buttons to press with her. I knew how to easily wrap her around my finger, where her strengths and weaknesses laid. Josefine was an incredibly empathetic and kind-hearted person who was always concerned that the people she loved were doing well.

She would do anything for those she let into her heart, and that was a wonderful prerequisite for me. It was both her greatest forté and her greatest downfall. She would always put the welfare of her loved ones above her own. She wasn't someone who always had to please everyone, but she was always careful not to hurt anyone. I knew that the boundaries she set for herself and others were therefore sometimes blurred. I knew what I had to say to win Josefine over.

"Lil, say something. Please say you're not angry with me! I just don't want anything to happen to either one of us. I just want to protect us"

With that I had her wrapped around my little finger, I could see it on her face even before her lips parted and she uttered the words.

"You are right. And I really appreciate the fact that you put our well-being above not having to keep us a secret. We'll do as you say"

I had called it.

Josefine was intelligent, but also a good person, which made her incredibly predictable.

Josefine

I was happy. I was finally in a relationship again. It had taken long enough. The last time I had been in a relationship, things had ended anything but beautifully. I had pulled out of the dating life for a year because I felt like I needed to regain my footing. My ex-girlfriend had been possessive, and Jane had always warned me that she was just taking advantage of me. How right she had been. But I didn't listen to her back then, so the end of that relationship had left me devastated.

After that year, I had always wanted to start dating again, but it had never really worked out. I hadn't been on a single date in the last three years.

And now I had a new partner. It felt nice, flattering, to be wanted by someone. And I liked her too. I couldn't wait until my stomach pain finally subsided, but it only seemed to get worse. I put it down to the fact that I was certainly very excited about this very pleasant situation.

I looked at my mobile phone and Jane's face was still there. We simply hadn't wanted to end our video call, so we were now co-existing and doing our thing, with the warming presence of each other by our side.

She was folding a huge pile of laundry and when she noticed me looking at her, she gave me a dirty grin.

She then sank her hand into the sea of fabric and when she looked at me again, she was holding an indefinable black something in her hand. "Guess what this is?" I shrugged my shoulders. "How should I know?" I asked, adding ironically, "A sock? Ewwww..."

She laughed. "Gosh Lil... it's a thong. You'll have to wait until the second date to see it on though"

Punch in the stomach. Nausea. I felt like I had just been defeated in a boxing match by several opponents. I felt uncomfortable when she said something like that. I knew I shouldn't feel that way in this situation. I should feel a thousand butter-flies tingling, but if I was honest with myself, I didn't. Which didn't necessarily mean that I wasn't in love with Jane. It just meant that I needed time to adapt to the new situation. Nothing more, nothing less. I put on a mock-offended face and re-plied "Oh, that's too bad..."

After that, I did everything I could to change the subject as quickly as possible, which meant that our phone call ended al-most immediately.

Jane

Josefine was too unenthusiastic from my point of view! I had to make her really believe that she loved me.

I wanted to be with her more than anything, and it was important that she thought she wanted the same thing. I had to somehow manage to get even further into her head. I had spent the whole last year slowly but surely changing her mind.

I had shown her that I was the only true friend of hers. I had made sure that she didn't trust anyone as much as she trusted me. I had badmouthed everyone else until there was only me in Josefine's inner circle. Me, and only me. There was virtually no escape for her, she couldn't get away from me because I was her only social anchor that saved her from complete isolation. I was good for her, she knew that. I was always there for her, and she could trust me. I was the only one Josefine had, and now it was time for her to make amends.

She had to pay me back for the many hours I had spent lovingly deconstructing and cleaning out her entire social life. Only I deserved her, only I should own her. I had done her a favour and now she had to prove her gratitude by loving me in return. I would get her to think that she was loving this. Oh dear, she was so kind, and at the same time so naive. So easy to manipulate...

How good that I protected her. I wouldn't let anyone take advantage of her, manipulate her, abuse her.

The doorbell rang at my flat. "Josefine!" was my first thought, but I realised it wasn't her before I even pressed the door handle and invited my guest in.

It was Soleil... who else would it be?

In her hand she held a bouquet of flowers, lilies, my favourite. Lilies, like Lil, my nickname for Josefine. "Hi" Soleil sounded downright shy "I thought I'd drop by and see how you're doing... To be honest... I'm a bit overwhelmed... I don't know how to... deal with the situation... you know... I've never experienced anything like this before and I want to be there for you, but... I don't want to do anything wrong either..." Her voice trembled. "Mhh" my tone sounded harsher than I intended. She had disturbed me, pulled me out of my thoughts about Josefine, and now I was forced to talk badly about her, about the love of my life. I was dripping with contempt inside, but I had to make sure I got my emotions under control as quickly as possible, otherwise I would just give myself away. "For God's sake, Jane, please don't get me wrong!" There was despair in her eyes. Those eyes, so full of emotion. She was getting on my nerves.

"I want to be there for you, I am just terrified to overstep your boundaries. I've spent all night on the internet trying to figure out the best way to help you... I just want you to be okay. Please tell me as soon as I do something you're not comfortable with, okay?"

"My favourite thing would be for you never to touch me again, enter my flat or be anywhere near me" I refrained from commenting, as I was concerned about my university degree. The next few hours passed slowly as Soleil *actually* tried to make plans on how to help me the best. And I, I sat there, listening, nodding at one point or another, with a blank look in my eyes, and Soleil felt vindicated. Actually, my lack of emotion was due to the fact that I was bored and Soleil's sheer presence bothered me, but I let her believe that the reason for my behaviour was a profoundly traumatic event. I liked this role, I was the victim in her eyes, and she was a respectful human being. She wouldn't even dream of touching me in a romantic way any time soon.

Soleil was bursting with such empathy and energy that she was too much for me. She was too demanding and she got on my nerves, but her character was definitely useful for this situation. I didn't have to do much acting to get her to believe me, I didn't have to say much to get her to do what I wanted her to do, I had her trapped under my fingertip. Soleil was intelligent, but she was also emotional, and that made it so much easier for me to keep her under control.

I realised that the role of the abuse victim was especially working for Soleil. In addition to her incredibly huge and incredibly nerve-wracking empathy, she had her own experiences with the subject. When we first met, she had told me about how she had been raped by a friend when she was a teenager. She had told me in detail how it had happened, how she had felt, and I had been able to recognise the pain in her eyes. When she had spoken of rape at the time, I had felt sympathy, but when she told me her story, I secretly had to admit to myself that I thought she was overdramatising things. She had spoken of chronic periods of pain that had plagued her for years, of periods when she could hardly eat, of periods when she had only been able to lie in bed and stare at the ceiling motionlessly. "I was dead, except my body was alive", she had said, and I had looked at her and nodded, thinking to myself "what some people make up in order to get attention" Back then, I hadn't really cared about this grotesqueness that Soleil carried with her, because I had loved her and I hadn't cared that she sometimes overdramatised things.

I didn't love her anymore.

I was annoyed by her hypocritical way of being there for me. She wasn't as nice as she pretended to be, I'd wager. I would never behave like that, and I really wasn't a bad person.
"I have to be honest with you Jane, I have the utmost respect for you, the way you're getting through this difficult situation." Shit! My mind had drifted. Soleil looked at me piercingly, so much love in her gaze that I was disgusted. "I wasn't so good at coping with my situation back then. You're really

strong" I wasn't the least bit in the mood for her sentimental ramblings, so I looked at her, deeply hurt, and asked "Are you saying I'm lying?" As expected, she looked at me in shock. "No, Jane, no. For God's sake! I believe you. I wanted to encourage you and I wanted to tell you that everything will be all right again one day!"

Josefine

I was drained. I wanted to sleep, I just wanted to lie down in my bed and close my eyes. I needed rest, but every time I gave in to my physical desire for a break, every time I tried to relax my muscles and fall asleep, the thoughts in my head became unbearably loud. It was quiet around me, and while my eyes were open and I was distracted, I was able to function to a certain extent, but when I tried to give my body the break, the relaxation it deserved, an avalanche of thoughts erupted from my head. I tried my best to think said thoughts so that they would leave my head and grant me my peace, but whenever I tried to grasp one of my thought fibres, it immediately escaped from my mind.

It was as if my head was full of everything and nothing at the same time.

I realised that I wasn't going to get anywhere on my own at this point. I needed to talk to a friend. Under normal circumstances, I would have turned up at Jane's, asked her for advice, let her give me a hug, but unfortunately, given the situation, that wasn't an option.

Who else could I ask? Who could I go to? Who would I not bother with my presence? Was there anyone at all who I would not annoy? I knew that I wasn't an uncomplicated person. I was too much of everything, too happy, too sad, too empathetic. Generally, too much. I held up too much space.

I didn't have many friends, and since I had met Jane, I wasn't really as intimate with anyone else as I was with her.

I didn't have to disguise myself in front of Jane, didn't have to filter what I said, didn't have to decimate my emotions to a 'normal' amount. In other words, I could just be myself, the real me, the me that I was in my head, and not the image I was trying to embody while I was around people I didn't feel as safe with. Mentally, I went through people who were in my immediate social circle and got stuck on Harper. I considered her one of my best friends, but we had been much closer in the past. Today we still knew each other very well, but since I had become closer with Jane, our friendship had drifted a little out of sight. I was a horrible person! Jane was so right. How could I even consider burdening her with my sensitivities when I had just lied to her face about a minor matter? Besides, it had been me who had let our friendship slide. It was my fault that we were no longer inseparable. I didn't deserve her in my life. I...

I hated it when my head did that. Whenever I panicked, my first instinct was to look for a problem within myself, my second was to apologise profusely to everyone and their mother for the most absurd things. I was just like that. I had it under control for a long time, but for the past year, it had become much stronger again. The only person who was able to pull me off my mental tangle was Jane. She had a lot of power over me. I was grateful to know that she was a good person and would never take advantage of it. I made a decision. Harper liked me. She had always stuck with me, and we had been through ups and downs in our friendship. I could talk to her. She wouldn't judge me, whether I deserved it or not was something else. Before I could afford to brood over something like that again, I first had to make sure I was able to think again. I picked up my mobile phone from the coffee table and dialled Harper's number. After the second ring, the dialling tone beeped from the other end.

"Hello?"

"Hi, Harper"

"Josefine? Is that you?"

"It's me, and I'm in a mess... I'm not really allowed to tell anyone... but... do you have time to talk to me? I... think I need your advice"

"Of course, of course! Do you want to come over?"

"Thanks, you're the best. See you in a bit!"

Harper's flat was only a block away from mine.

When I arrived at her front door, I felt sick, but it was a different kind of pain than the last few days. I realised how my guilty conscience seemed to be eating me up inside.

Harper was so kind and loving towards me. And I... I was... well, *me*.

I was me, and she deserved such a better friend.

Before I even had a chance to ring the doorbell, I heard the buzz of the door and stepped inside. Harper's flat was on the third floor, and when I got upstairs, she was already standing on the staircase, ready to hug me.

A few minutes later, we were sitting together on her couch, holding two cups of chai tea and a shot of white wine each.

I was one of these people who didn't really drink alcohol, but I realised that this conversation was going to be awkward. I would have to speak my truth, and I wasn't even sure what my truth actually was.

"How are you?" The look in Harper's eyes was honest "How can I help you?"

At first, I didn't know what to say. Yes, good question... What was actually going on? How was I feeling? I closed my eyes, took a deep breath and saw Jane in my mind's eye. I saw her and I heard her voice, I heard her words. 'Bad girlfriend' echoed inside me again and again.

And suddenly everything blurted out of me. At that moment, everything became too much to bear. "I'm so sorry! I'm a terrible friend" I saw the astonishment on Harper's face. She started to say something, but I wasn't able to stop. "I let our friendship slide and as soon as I have a problem I come back to you. I'm a bad person, I'm so sorry! But I really do love you, please believe me! You're always there, even though I don't deserve it. You're an angel!"

Harper looked at me, still perplexed, but with a soft

expression in her eyes. She stared at the wall for a bit before she started to speak. She always did that, she thought. That's why I enjoyed talking to her so much. The words that came out of her mouth were well thought out. She thought before she spoke, and she always did her best to be helpful. I really appreciated that about her.

"I know you, and I know this isn't personal. You've got a lot going on at the moment and that's absolutely fine. We have a wonderful friendship and it's perfectly normal that we don't see each other that often sometimes. A friendship like ours has to be able to put up with that"

"Oh Harper, you're an angel! Thank you so much. What would I do without you?"

"Not at all, sweetheart. Not for that. But you said something about a misery. Would you like to tell me what's going on there?"

"If I knew that so well"

"Okay... it's about a person, right?"

"Yes... no, yes"

"Do I know him or her, is it a he or a she?"

"It's a she and yes, no. Damn. I have no idea. Actually, there is no problem at all. At most, I am the problem. Oh, just forget it. Jane didn't do anything wrong"

"Jane? Our Jane?" Harper sounded interested, but she didn't push me to say anything. With her I had the feeling that I could say exactly the things that I felt comfortable with.

"Yes, Jane. But it's stupid. My head is just overdramatizing things again that are actually quite normal. But I've been feeling really bad since it happened, and I can barely eat."

"It doesn't sound to me as if there was nothing. Would you like to explain to me what you mean by 'it'? If you have quarrelled, then I can promise you that everything will become better eventually. Honestly, you two are the best of friends after all. You girls are going to make up for it"

"No, we didn't argue. Oh, God. Actually, I really shouldn't tell this to anyone at all. I'm such a horrible person."

"You're not. Everyone needs to talk about things that keep them up at night sometimes. This is quite normal. And don't worry. I'm not going to tell on you "

"I don't know, just like that, behind Jane's back...?"

"Is it something that concerns you?"

Harper asked just the right questions. She would one day become a brilliant psychologist; I was sure of that.

"Yes, it concerns me I believe."

"You see... if it concerns you, then you can also talk about it. That's your decision!"

"So... Jane and I... We-We're probably a couple now?"

"A couple? Honestly, you don't sound so fond of that"

"We are involved because unfortunately she liked our kiss quite well"

Unfortunately? Why, did I say unfortunately? I was with her. I should be happy about that. Was I completely nuts now?

"Your kiss? But I thought you've been friends?"

"Yes, we were... she's my best friend"

"Correct me if I'm wrong, but don't you actually have this rule... how was it... Friendship remains friendship and relationship remains relationship?"

"Yes, that's my rule. I think it's impressive that you remember that"

"Josefine, you are distracting from the topic. Of course, I remember the things you say, you are one of my closest friends, but I'm afraid I don't quite understand how your kiss initiated then"

"That was not my decision"

"What do you mean by that? How was it not your decision? Otherwise, whose decision should it be?"

"Well, Janes. I said no, because I didn't think the idea was so brilliant, but well... she just kissed me anyway"

"You said no?"

"Yes, of course, several times. You said you remembered my rule?"

"Have I understood this correctly now. You said no, *multiple times*, and she kissed you anyway?"

„Exactly. She kissed and touched me. She just won..."

"Won? Josefine, do you know what that is?"

"What do you mean?" I was confused. I didn't understand why there was suddenly a troubled look in her eyes.

"Finchen, this is abuse?!"

Oh, come on... Harper saw this too closely. Jane was my friend. She would never- she just wanted the best for me, and she was in love with me.

"For God's sakes, Harper! Jane would never-"

"Think about it, what else is it supposed to be. Please stop protecting her!"

"She is my friend. She loves me, she would never do anything that could hurt me"

"Josefine, friends don't do that kind of thing"

"But she loves me!"

"Do you love her?"

"Platonically, I'm afraid" I'm a terrible person. I denied my girlfriend, who I should actually consider myself lucky to have. I was a disgusting little brat...

"Then break up!" Harper's words hit me like an arrow. I couldn't- I couldn't break up.

"Jane didn't deserve this. I would be a bad friend if I wasn't with her. I don't deserve her either way, but at least I can do her a little justice that way."

"Finchen, you're impossible right now. You can't be serious?! You are a wonderful person, and everyone can consider themselves lucky to have you, but a relationship is about love. You deserve to be in a relationship with someone *you* love"

"Do you think she will hate me?"

"No, Josefine. You can't do anything about your feelings. Do yourself the favour and break up with her. If you need me, I'll help you with that"

"I think I have to do this alone. Thanks Harper. You are an angel. I don't know what I would do without you."

"Don't be so hard on yourself, Josefine"

Josefine

After some time, the conversation between me and Harper got lost, and with the words "You can do it, I believe in you" she sent me home.

When I arrived at my apartment, this feeling of emptiness overwhelmed me again, but I just couldn't buckle under it. I had to do it. I had to do what was right. When I picked up my phone, an almost consuming fear pushed aside my feeling of apostasy. What remained was me, as a trembling pile of misery, huddled in my bed. My phone in my hand.

I opened the WhatsApp text field and started typing.

"Dear Jane,

I've been thinking about how and whether to tell you, but I must be honest with you…

I didn't mean to hurt you when you told me that you felt more then platonically for me, and to be honest, I also thought that maybe my feelings could grow if we saw each other more often. Besides, it was very flattering to be told such a thing. But I've noticed that it wouldn't be fair to you to continue to pretend that I have more than just friendly feelings towards you. I realized for myself that my feelings towards you are different than, for example, for my ex-girlfriend at that time. It is very difficult for me to write this message to you, because I really do not want to hurt you in any case. I hope that you can understand this, and we can still remain friends as you said. Friends who can trust each other with everything, and who are there for each other, because I think we are a really good team. I definitely don't want you to be sad now. You don't have to text me back directly if you don't feel like it, but if you need an open ear, then I'm there"

I had poured my whole heart into this message. I had meant everything last bit of it. It had felt good in a way to have been so honest, even if the voice inside me screamed more loudly than ever that I was a terrible person. I pressed "send" and barely two minutes later I was able to read an answer on my screen.

"Okay" was written there. Nothing more, no punctuation mark, nothing. „Okay"

Somehow that was the worst answer I could have gotten. Not because it was scratching at my ego, but because I knew Jane, and knew it wasn't true. She wasn't *okay*.

"What do you say?", I answered.

"Have you been playing theatre lately?"

"Well...I really like you, and it's also true that I appreciate the time with you, but... not like that"

"Well played! I actually bought it from you. Applause"

"I just didn't want to hurt you. I'm sorry!!!"

I was desperate.

Jane

And boom, I had Josefine wrapped around my finger. How easy it was. Of course, it scratched at my ego that I probably didn't have her in my clutches as deeply as I thought, but in this situation, the opportunity to change this was thankfully offered.

"I'm not mad at you" I wrote.

"Really?"

"Don't worry," I grinned. Now I had her trapped. She would worry, and I would dismiss her.

"I will, though. I don't want you to be sad"

"It's okay"

"It's not"

"Then let's unfortunately remain friends"

"As long as you write, unfortunately, not everything has been cleared yet"

"What are you going to do?!", a little anger, a little played hurt. That was the perfect recipe to tie Josefine to me. Her empathy was her biggest weakness, and I loved it when I managed to use it for myself.

"Just tell me if you don't want to talk about it right now"

"Yes, sure, then let's talk, but what are you going to do?"

"Keep texting you until you feel better."

Now that I had her on the hook, it was time for my final move. I closed WhatsApp and switched my phone to airplane mode. Voilá, a good deed every day.

Josefine

After Jane had not answered for a suspiciously long time, I wrote again "Jane?"

My message didn't go through anymore. I had the feeling that I had just made the biggest mistake of my life. Had I lost the person who meant the most to me in this world?

That night I did not close my eyes, and the sleepless night, chased me into a disastrous day.

When I saw Jane walking through the university in the morning, just the sight of her was enough to make me burst into tears.

The first time I met Soleil, I was standing in front of the girl's bathrooms' mirror, trying my best not to burst into tears again. I knew her by sight, she was an English studies major, so I believed. When she entered, the look from her deep blue eyes was pinned onto me. It wasn't a passing glance. No curious sniffing. She knew me, she knew who I was, and she wanted something from me.

Too bad that I still felt as if I was going to burst into tears as soon as I opened my mouth.

My world had collapsed several times in the last few days, and I had no idea how to deal with this situation.

She was standing in front of me, looking at me, I was looking at her. Inappropriately, it struck me how beautiful she was. Two braids peeked out from under her beanie, she was smaller than me, slim but still muscular. Her freckled face was perfectly formed, but her initially only intense gaze now seemed threatening. There was no kindness in her expression. Oh, please don't, not someone who was out to argue. My nerves couldn't stand this today.

So far I had only looked at her through the mirror, but now I turned towards her. "If you're having a bad day, I'm sorry for you, but I'm really not in the mood for arguing right now" I said, but when the words left my mouth, I almost didn't recognize my voice. I sounded dull, as if all energy had left my body. I sounded how I felt.

But either she didn't seem to notice this fact, or she didn't care, because she continued to look at me pokingly, her gaze dripping with contempt.

"After all, do you regret what you did? Do you regret it", she sounded rough, as if she, too, was crying.

I was so confused that for a short moment I forgot about my current situation. "Come again please?" I was struck. This situation could not get any more absurd. A total stranger looked at me with a gaze, as if I had eaten her cat, and asked me if I regretted "it" whatever "it" was.

In fact, a lot of things occurred to me at the moment that I wish had never happened, but none of these things involved in any way the strange girl who was standing in front of me right here, right now and seemed to seriously demand an answer.

"After all, do you regret what you did? ", the same question, only this time her voice was noticeably colder.

"Honestly, I really don't have the nerve for something like this right now, sorry" I slowly started to get annoyed.

"I don't have the faintest idea who you are and what you want from me, but I think you're confusing me"

"You are Josefine"

"Yes, but what do you want from me, and who are you anyway?"

"Don't play pretend!"

Slowly I was really close to losing my last string of patience. Whoever she was, I didn't know her, I hadn't done anything to her, so what should I regret about her?

"Who are you?", my voice was emphatically calm, but my effort to make it sound like that was just as clearly detectable.

"My name is Soleil"

Soleil, French for sun. Whenever I had met her in the hall-
ways, I would have described her as the sun as well. She had
always seemed happy; she had really shone. One had already
felt warm when they walked past her... the sun. But now she
was standing in front of me and seemed like "la lune", the
moon. Beautiful, and dark, and cold. I believed her that something had happened, and it hurt any empathy in me to see
that- whatever it was, had stolen her spark. Only I could not
help her, since I neither knew her, nor knew what could have
happened to her.
"Soleil, I don't know who you are and what has been done to
you. Whatever it is, I'm honestly sorry for you, but I really
don't know you. I don't have the faintest idea who you are or
what to do with you. If you like to talk, we can go for a coffee,
but otherwise I honestly can't help you"
She kept staring at me but said nothing anymore.
Normally, I would have continued to take care of her, but I
was in a terrible state, my whole body ached and I could
hardly look straight ahead.
So, I waited a few more seconds to see if she wanted to say anything still, and when she remained silent, I started to move
past her out of the door, out into the corridor.
When I took the latch in my hand, I felt a hand on my arm and
pulled it back like a flash, as if I had burned myself. I wish
with all my heart that I had been able to react more calmly,
not to seem like a terrified deer, but physical contact was unbearable for me under the current circumstances.
There was still the same hatred in Soleil's gaze.
"You disgust me!" She paused for a moment, seemed to be
looking for words, trying not to punch me "Someone like you
does not deserve to walk around freely. You are supposed to
be locked up, you sick psycho!" With these words, she turned
around and disappeared into one of the stalls.
I stopped, completely perplexed and in a way hurt. I tried to

realize what had just happened, but with all my heart, I wasn't able to bring any sense into this conversation.

I shook my head, as if I could shake off the strange feeling that the interaction with Soleil had left inside me.

All the way home, I was accompanied by the look with which she had pierced me before she turned away from me. No matter how much I was pondering, I didn't get what had just happened. Focusing my thoughts on what was wrong with others was therapeutic in a way, because it gave me a short break, a little distraction from what was actually going on in my life right now.

When I got home, I tried to text Jane again. After all, she had said that we could be friends if our relationship didn't work out. I missed her with all my heart. Harper might be right about a lot of things she said, but I just couldn't believe that Jane would...Never, no…

Harper was certainly wrong. Abuse... That was a serious accusation. Jane would never do that. That was- mentally I apologized to Harper- that was bullshit.

Jane loved me more than anything, she was even in love with me, feelings that I did not return, but she *loved* me. You would never hurt someone you love. I stood behind this statement with my entire existence. Loving someone meant that you were only doing well yourself if the other person was doing well. One suffered when the other did.

And Jane... Jane loved me.

Ergo, she couldn't have done anything to me at all, because that would have gone against the principle of love.

I took out my phone and opened WhatsApp.

I stared blankly at the text field. I knew exactly what I wanted to say, but I didn't have the words for it.

"Hey," I typed. But this is where my range of expertise ended. With all due respect, how was one to start a conversation like this?

"I miss you. Do you think we can be friends again, like before, like you said?"

That was... direct, but maybe that was the best way.

I pressed send.

It did not take a minute before Jane had opened my message. I felt my pulse increase and I was barely able to breathe. Her answer would emboss my future. The truth was, I had no idea who I was without Jane. She was a huge and irreversible part of my life. If she was suddenly missing, it was like painting a picture with a brush and canvas, but without paint.

"I need you in my life, but you will never be just a friend to me"

Jane's message hit me like a punch in the pit of my stomach. I had no idea what to say, because she, too, was so incredibly important to me, but my love for her purely platonic.

I hesitated, started typing "Do you think we can try it out? You are incredibly important to me"

But even before I had the chance to send my reply, another one of Jane's messages materialised on my screen. At the sight of it, all air left my lungs.

"I'm sorry to tell you this Josefine, but I think I can't live without you, and I don't want to either"

"But you don't have to live without me. I will always be there for you, and I will always love you"

I had never typed so fast in my life. My heart was racing, and I started to see the letters of my mobile phone keyboard twice. My whole environment was spinning and I was swaying.

"Josefine, I have made my decision. Don't lie, because you don't love me. You never loved me, neither romantically nor platonically"

How did she come up with this? What had I done wrong? Why wasn't I a good friend? Should I have told her more often that I loved her? Was every night not enough? Should I have hugged her tighter? I wish I had hugged her tighter, the last time we saw each other. Would that have changed anything? Would she have been happier then?

"Jane... that's not true. Maybe I haven't told you this often enough, but I've always loved you, and I still do. You're the best friend I've ever had, and I love you, I *need* you!"

The blue hooks at the bottom right corner of my message remained blue for far too long. Blue, but unanswered. I was getting nauseous. Had she? Did she?

No!

Jane

I laughed. Loud, angry. I had her tangled up. Josefine had drawn exactly the conclusions I wanted her to draw.

I had only had to scatter her tiny breadcrumbs, and now she was sitting where I wanted her to be; in my trap!

Of course I didn't want to kill myself. How naive was she, like please? And who did she actually think she was? Kill me because of *her*…

As if she was resistant in any way. If I wanted her, I could still have her. I still wanted her. She was hot, she was nice, and she was mine. I had her in my hands, and at some point she would buckle down and realize that she liked me too. And then... then she would be grateful to me for all that I had done for us.

I had to make sure that Soleil didn't come to the university campus tomorrow, otherwise my plan wouldn't work out. But first I had to calm Josefine down enough so that she could hold out until the next morning.

"My mind is made up" I typed.

I saw her reading my message right away, so I took a few seconds to catch up. "Let's talk in front of the university tomorrow" I wanted her to panic. I wanted to take up all the space in her head, but I didn't want her to show up here or even call an ambulance.

"Certainly, Jane, please promise me that you won't hurt yourself!" Lol, naive, little Josefine. But good for me, nice that she cut to that topic. "Cut" I smirked. My word jokes were macabre, but at least they were funny.

"I can't promise anything" I typed. "Maybe I won't be able to do it without the blade under my watch"

I could see in my mind's eye how Josefine turned chalky white. Maybe she even ran to the bathroom to throw up. I loved my power, and she gave me more and more of it...

voluntarily. How nice she was. "But I'll tell you one thing. If you show up here today, or call the ambulance, then I'll be dead faster than you can help me"

Blue checkmarks. Josefine's answer amounted to a few words. "I love you. You are strong"

How sweet... she actually thought that would change something. Well ... at least she meant well.

I closed our chat and opened the one with Soleil.

How did I best get her to stay off my neck tomorrow? She was so terribly affectionate, so terribly caring.

"Hey honey" I shove and pretended that I had to suppress a gag reflex. My smile about my own comedy echoed in my body.

Hey honey... how she took me seriously when I wrote something like that was the biggest mystery to me. Almost as good as "Hey babe" Or " Hey poockie". Pathetic! So pathetic, but also so funny. I made a mental note that as soon as I ever used such a phrase seriously, someone should please throw a microwave at my head. Only people who had to beg for relationships said something like that. People no one wanted, people who couldn't have everyone, like I could. In other words, Soleil, or Josefine...

Stop, stop. I couldn't get distracted now. I had to arrange everything for tomorrow. I smirked. Tomorrow was showdown. Tomorrow would come the day that I had been carefully preparing for so long.

"Hey honey. Can you do me a favour tomorrow morning?"
Soleil read my message immediately. Since I had told her that Josefine had abused me, she was always there within half a minute maximum. She reacted to a whistle like a well-trained dog.

"Of course! What is it babe?"
Babe... this time I laughed out loud, loud and shrill and throaty. My point about these words was proven.

"I have an incredibly important lecture tomorrow morning. But I have to pick up a prescription from my doctor. Do you think maybe you could..."

"Certainly! Will you tell me when and where?"

"That's where a little bit of the problem is. The office is about an hour from here. If that's too much to ask I'll just skip the lecture"

I already knew her answer even before she started typing. With my last sentence I had her secured.

"God no! If it is important, then do not skip it. My lecture tomorrow morning if from a friend of my father. That'll work out. I'm driving for you"

I had known it after all. How easy my life was because of Soleil's and Josefine's character.

I could consider myself lucky if I didn't know that I was the one who had shaped them like this.

I was their God; I was their Creator. They were my creations, so I also had the right to direct them. They should be grateful that I did, because what would they be doing without me anyway?

I smiled at myself before I went to bed and fell asleep. Tomorrow would be epic.

Josefine

I had never gotten ready that quickly in the morning. Well, I hadn't had the chance to be sleepy either, because that implied that I had been sleeping.

In the meantime, I had taught myself how to take a blind shower. It was like an automated process. If I could not identify the problem and solve it, I had to adapt.

Only this abdominal pain was about to steal my last nerve. I could not contain it, neither with medication nor otherwise. Nothing seemed to work, which really made it difficult for me to accept it.

When I entered the campus, I saw it from afar. I didn't see what, I didn't see who, but I saw that something seemed to be going on in front of the main building.

A considerable crowd of people had formed on the stairs in front of the main entrance. As I approached, I saw that everyone seemed to be staring upwards, captivated by what was happening there. I slowly followed their gaze, and my heart stopped for a few seconds. I felt sick, and my already pale skin tone, which was characterized by the fatigue and stress of the last few days dimmed by another nuance.

On the roof- dangerously close to the edge, stood Jane. I stopped thinking and started acting. I ran around the crowd, past the building, until I stopped at the side entrance. I opened the door and made my way up the ferry stairs towards the roof. My side stung, my stomach ached, I suffered from double vision, which was probably due to how little I had eaten and slept.

But all this didn't matter now, the only thing that mattered was Jane. Jane. Jane!

Two more floors. One. There was the roof. A few more steps. I saw her right away. I was able to save her. I would save her. I would tear her away from the edge. She wouldn't throw herself down there. I would prevent it. I would save her. I wanted to save her. I had to save her.

If she died today, then it was my fault. Me and my stupid feelings. Maybe I loved her after all. Maybe, I just hadn't realized it until now. Maybe I had been too blind, too stupid, to see that Jane was right, that we belonged together.

And now her life was in danger. My fault. My fault. My fault! These words ate into my heart while I was crossing the roof at a sprint pace. It was my fault. My fault, my fault, *because of me!* Three more steps to Jane. She seemed to hear me now, turned to me and smiled broadly. She took another step towards the abyss. Oh god! Abyss. I could have vomited on the spot. Abyss! I had to prevent it. What was I doing here? I was too slow. I wasn't fast enough. Not enough. I didn't love her enough, I wasn't fast enough, *my fault.*

I had arrived. There she was. I locked her in both my arms and let myself drop backwards to the ground with full force. The collision with the roof was hard. Her elbow bumped into the pit of my stomach, and her weight made colliding with the roofing feel even more painful. I turned around, laid on top of her, fixed her with my body so that she could not get up, could not get to the edge, not to the edge of the roof, not to this damn abyss.

Only now, when I heard Jane fidgeting under me, I realized that we were touching. There was no other way. Somehow I had to save her. I realized the tight feeling in my throat too late to suppress it. Jane's body so close to mine gave me the rest. The black dots in front of my eyes were no longer just dots, first they were spots, then blobs, then they took up almost my entire screen area.

I heard footsteps approaching. Loud footsteps. And scream. I heard shouting sounds, but in my twilight state I could not make out the spoken words.

I felt some hands grabbing my waist, they pushed me away,

they pushed me away from Jane. "No" I shouted, overcome by an incredible panic. "She wants to jump. I have to save her"
Screaming again, again I did not understand what was said. Only loud screams and darkness that echoed in my head.
"No" I shouted again. Then "Jane"
"No, no, no!", a whimper left my mouth, but it didn't sound like I was talking, it wasn't me, it wasn't my voice. I didn't want to talk, I didn't want to whimper. I had to be strong, I had to save Jane.

I felt the hand again. I felt her under my arms as she pulled me to my feet. That voice again. The new voice that had just joined us. Again, she said something, and she seemed familiar to me. From somewhere? From where? From where? From where?

Who was she? It was important. Would she help Jane? Or would she end up conjuring up the disaster? Would she let Jane jump?

I felt pain. I didn't know where. Where I felt pain. I had to locate it. Did I fall off the roof? No! I still felt the ground beneath my feet. Again, the screaming, again, the voice, again, *this* voice? From where? Who?

The pain! My cheek. My cheek hurt. Whoever the voice was, she had given me a slap across the face.

Suddenly everything became clearer. I still didn't see anything, but now I could clearly hear what the voice was saying. Soleil's voice. "Your fault!"

Or was that my voice. My inner voice. She was right eighter way. It was my fault. I had dumped Jane. I had been insensitive. I didn't deserve her. I loved her and I had spoiled it. I had not adhered to my own principle.

"Why did you rape her?"

Uh- what? I was so blown away that everything stopped. My vision became clearer again, and Soleil's face materialized in front of my eyes. Pained with anger.

"You disgusting asshole!" She took another step towards me. I could feel her breath on my face.

"You raped my girlfriend. She wants to kill herself now because of you. You're so disgusting. It always has to be about you. You narcissist. And now you're acting like you're trying to save her. You destroyed her. You don't care about her. You disgusting bitch!"

With these words, she turned around and spoke to the rescue workers. Rescue workers? Rescue workers?!

When did they arrive here? Since when have there been rescue workers here? Good, Good, Very good! There were rescuers here, Jane needed rescuers. They would help Jane. Jane would be sent to the hospital. At the hospital, they would *help* Jane. Help.

But what did that have to do with this Soleil? She was a mystery to me? First this situation in the girls bathroom, and now she was here too?

And girlfriend? She called Jane her girlfriend? She had gone crazy, crazy, beside herself. Jane loved me, that was probably clear after this disaster. So what did girlfriend mean? And what did this girl come up with? I have raped Jane? No way. No way. N.E.V.E.R!

I would never do anything that could hurt Jane. Yes, I had broken up with her. But I would never do it on purpose. I would never touch her if she said no-

...said no. I would never kiss Jane if she said no-

I only realized that I had started moving when I had already left the roof and had almost finished the stairs.

I would never- no!

No-Jane; No.

But she... me.

I had said no. No-

Jane had kissed me. She had-

My body- but I had said no.

Said no- but nevertheless there were her hands-
Her hands on my body. No. No! No-
Was Harper…? No Harper couldn't be right-
Harper wasn't right!

I started running. I was running through the park of the university campus. My feet led my way towards the city hospital on their own.

I had to talk. Talk to Jane.

I had to ask her. She would know. I didn't know. Did she abuse me, rape me? Had she heard that I had said no. But I had said it several times. Maybe two times no meant yes. Maybe I hadn't been clear enough. Maybe I didn't understand some social context. It was my fault, for sure. Jane had done nothing wrong. How could I have had such a thought for even a second?!

Jane was feeling bad, not me.

Jane wanted to kill herself, not me.

Jane was suffering from the situation, *not me.*

I was the problem, *not Jane.*

My poor Jane. My thoughts were a crime. I had to be punished. I belonged locked up.

How could I have insinuated such a nuisance to Jane? How could I. How terrible, terrible of a human I was.

I didn't deserve her. I didn't deserve her love. Why did she love me so much? What did she see in me? And why was I so arrogant not to love her back.

I was a selfish cripple, and if she was already dating down, scooping down to me, to my level, who did I think I was to refuse her. She was so much better than me. She would never accuse me of something like that. And there I was. Disgusting. Agitating. Repulsive.

I didn't deserve Jane, only the poor woman couldn't know that. She could not look into my head. She did not see how disrespectful my thoughts were towards her.

I am a horrible disgusting person. Soleil had been right. But with everything? Had she been right about everything in the end?

Had I raped Jane? She didn't want our kiss? Didn't she want our kiss?

But she had- She had been the one who-

Stop! Was that victim blaming? How did I dare to do to decide if she had wanted to kiss me. Fact was that I did not reciprocate her feelings. Did she want to kiss someone who didn't love her? Had I abused her because she had kissed me without me loving her? Had she kissed me- had I kissed her? Did that even make a difference?

Did it? Were there any differences? Gradations? Was I less of a monster when she kissed me than when I did it with her?

Did I say no? Or, in the end, it was her.

I was standing at the door of the hospital. I was standing there. It was in front of me. Looked down at me menacingly, and its cold grey concrete facade screamed "rapist".

I was afraid to enter. I was still nauseous, but I had to know. I had to hear it from her. I had to hear it from her mouth what I had done to her. I had to hear what a monster I was, what a horrible person.

I was standing at the door of the room that the friendly nurse had told me was Jane's, but I was terrified to enter. What if not only Jane was waiting for me in the room, but also Soleil?

What if there was no living Jane waiting for me in this room, but one who had hanged herself on the string of her dropper? What if-

I had to stop with this eternal thought game if I wanted to enter this room today.

It was clear already what would happen as soon as I entered this room. The scene was solidified. Only I didn't know what I was going to burst into.

I raised my hand and knocked timidly on the door. Was it just

me, or did the hallway suddenly start spinning?

I was dizzy, but I had knocked.

I had knocked, now I had to enter. I took a deep breath, in and out, then I pushed the latch down.

When I entered, to my relief I saw a single room with no visitors in front of me, to my horror Jane was lying in bed. I had been aware she most likely would, but the sight disturbed me in a completely new way.

"Hey" I sounded choked, my voice was shaking.

To my surprise, a wide, almost crazy-looking grin appeared on Jane's face as soon as I entered the room.

There wasn't really much to see of the person who was so ill that she had just wanted to fall off the roof.

Or was I mistaken? Was it just a facade? People didn't necessarily show their mental illnesses... But I knew Jane inside and out. I saw the smallest details in their facial expressions and gestures, and I could interpret them correctly most of the time. Jane didn't look the least bit unhappy just now. There was not that tiny crease on her left eyebrow, like on the day her cat died. There was not that emptiness in her eyes, as on the day her last ex-boyfriend left her. She was not devastated. She wasn't even sad. On the contrary.

No matter how hard she tried to hide it, I saw it on the right corner of her mouth. A minimal dimple had formed there. She triumphed. For some incomprehensible reason, she triumphed.

But that couldn't be- Why should she, in this situation-?

"I knew you were coming, that's why I sent Soleil to get some coffee" the expression on Jane's face remained unchanged, and almost scared me a little. This had to be part of a disease. I remembered reading the other day that some people could fall into a manic happiness episode just before or after their suicide attempt. Was this one such case? Did the doctors know about this? I had to see a doctor-

81

"We don't need a doctor, I'm fine, if I'm completely honest"
It was as if she had guessed my thoughts. We definitely
needed a doctor. Fast-
"Sit down Josefine" she now sounded imperious. Everything
friendly had been lost from her voice.
"Are you... sure?" I was unsure. Did I do something wrong
when I listened to her. I definitely didn't want to make the sit-
uation worse. There was no way I wouldn't make it worse.
Would my presence alone make the situation worse?
"Sit down. Now!" Jane scared me.
I pulled a chair to her bed and took a seat hesitantly. "Alright,"
I felt as if I was back at school and in the principal's office.
"I can imagine you have some questions, dear" now her voice
was dripping with false kindness. The first time I had the feeling that maybe Jane wasn't as transparent as she pretended to
be. What was she up to? Was she calculating something, plan-
ning something or was she just pretending, and in reality was
manically-depressed and in constant and direct danger of
hurting herself? Doctor-
"Stay seated!", cold, that tone of command again.
"It almost seems as if you don't like me, Josefine. No, no, that
can't be. You like me, you love me, you just don't know it yet.
You are dependent on me. So damn dependent. I am your
drug, your fucking drug. You need me. And you, you're the
pathetic Crackie. Without me you are nothing! " her laughter
was shrill, and made me shrink together. Was there a noise at
the door? Whatever.
But I had made up my mind. Jane was manic. I couldn't take
this seriously. I couldn't let this hurt me. She didn't know
what she was saying.
She wouldn't let me get up. She wouldn't let me get up, but
maybe I managed to press that red button unobtrusively.
"Don't even think about it!" Jane had followed my gaze and
was now looking at me expectantly.

"D-Did I abuse... Did I abuse you... Like Soleil...Did I...Ab-Ab-Abuse you?"

Again, that laugh from Jane's side.

"It's a pity that Soleil was not part of my plan. If I had hired her, I could have credited myself with the laurels for this. Damn... how does one say so beautifully "Nobody is perfect", right?"

This situation sent shivers down my spine. Jane was apparently completely psychotic. What plan was she talking about? Was there a plan? Had I missed something?

"Oh Lil, take a breath, relax. You didn't abuse me. You simply wouldn't be able to do that away. You'd still be too weak for that, even if you wanted to. It's always been like this, I'm the strong one of us. I'm the one who gets what she wants. If anyone abused anybody, it was me"

My mouth was open. A part of me wanted to believe her, the rest did not. Believing her meant freeing me from my potential guilt. Not to do it, however, was the only right thing. She was not in her right senses.

"Josefine, you can definitely believe me. I'm clearer than you think. I'm not feeling bad, I've never felt bad. This situation here, it's all just part of a big game. And this game is life. And I have the strings in my hand, I have everything planned. I am God. I'm fucking God!"

My mouth was open. My blank fear was written all over my face. Jane seemed to lose all connection to reality.

"What do you mean by plan? ", in every syllable of my question, my uncertainty was clearly detectable.

"Because you are too pathetic, too stupid to understand otherwise, I'll explain it to you. Thank me, let's go peasants, thank me!"

I hesitated. Should I play along, or did I just confirm her further in her illusions. Would I hurt her more? Or would I help her more with giving in?

I decided on the latter. What else should I do. I was not a medical professional. I was not trained for such a thing. I studied psychology as a teacher in the first semester. After the basics I was out of knowledge.

"Thank you, thank you Jane"

She seemed satisfied. "All right..." she nodded pleasantly.

"When I met you, I fell in love with you. This presented me with two problems. Firstly, that you do not feel that way, secondly", her face took on a slightly disgusted expression "Soleil. My second problem was my annoying girlfriend Soleil, whom I can't get rid of if I want my degree, because- dramatic irony, her father is my professor for my major"

I was too shocked to reply. A part of me still believed that Jane was slowly going mental, spiralling towards insanity, but an ever-increasing part doubted her mental state in a different way. She reminded me in some of her characteristics of a person with narcissistic personality disorder, if not a sociopath.

"Anyway" she sounded like she was telling me about her day quite frankly, and not about some kind of sadistic plan that involved me and her girlfriend (?!).

"I quickly found out that both you and Soleil have a common weakness. You are weak as soon as you love. And God, you are easy to manipulate. Sometimes I wish you would have made it a little harder for me." Again she laughed lightly, chuckling to herself. She somewhat took the form of a villain, who in the dramatic climax submitted all his perfidious plans to the hero...

In a strange way, this even corresponded to reality.

"I told Soleil that you abused me, just so she wouldn't touch me anymore. One less problem. Unfortunately, this has only made her more clingy and wanting to help me. Terrible thing isn't it?" My mouth was open.

"Well, and with you I could take whatever I wanted. Well,

what I wanted is easily said. It was what I deserved after all. I finally scooped down to your level, so it was only fair that I should be allowed to kiss you after all. I don't give a shit what you think about it, to be honest. You're not going to leave me anyway. You are nothing without me. You have got nothing without me. I still find it remarkable that you didn't notice how you had less and less contact with everyone else, and at some point, only I was there. And now no one wants you anymore but me. You need me. You're dead without me! "

I noticed how tears began to form in my eyes. *I* didn't realize yet what Jane had just explained to me; my body apparently did after all. A lonely tiny tear trickled out of my eye and landed in my lap, discolouring the fabric of my jeans at the spot where it hit.

"Why? ", my question was hardly a word, more a hint. Jane understood it anyway.

Her answer was short and cold *"Because I can Josefine, because I can"*

Soleil

I had been standing at the door. I had clung to the wall; at some point I had to hold on to it like my life was depending on it.

My whole world had collapsed. Nothing had been real. Jane didn't love me. I had only been a burden to Jane, at best perhaps a means to an end. I had understood why she had sent me to pick up a prescription for her today. She wanted to keep me out of the situation. The part of me that loved her wanted to scream that she wanted to protect me, but I knew that wasn't true.

Thankfully, Kathrin had called me, and thankfully I had been nearby.

But was it „thankfully"?

The part who still wanted to believe that Jane loved me, also preferred to be ignorant. I didn't want to hear what I actually meant to her.

And then there was my conscience.

Poor Josefine. She had been the victim, Jane's victim, and I had made her life even worse.

I remembered the situation in the bathroom of our university. She looked like she was at the verge of crying. And yet she had been kind to me. She even offered me her help. She was the one who needed help and I... I hadn't understood anything, had let Jane manipulate me to the point where I had lost my own judgment.

And now it was up to me to act. I decided to keep my attitude. I did what I did best and masked my emotions. I was deeply hurt, but there was only anger on my face, if at all. I opened the door and entered.

Without saying a word, I grabbed my bag with one hand, with the other I grabbed Josefine and pulled her out of the room with me.

I heard a silent "fuck", but I knew that Jane was not annoyed that she had lost me. It was the fact that her plan had gone wrong that bothered her.

In the hallway I really looked at Josefine for the first time since I knew her. It was undeniable, I saw what Jane saw in her. She was beautiful. Her face was almost symmetrical, only her left eyebrow looked like it was lifting slightly. Her cheekbones were accentuated, and her jawline was defined, but not so much that it seemed sharp. Everything about her was soft, tender... she had the traits of a fragile angel.

When I looked up close into her moist eyes, I saw that green was shining out of them. The colour of her iris was like dark amber with vivid green streaks.

She was adorable.

Wait- that wasn't what this was about right now. I was rude. I had been staring at her just like that for far too long.

"You're not mad, Soleil!" her voice sounded timid, vulnerable. "You can drop your facade in front of me. I'm not doing you any harm"

Damn it! Not one minute had passed and she already managed to read through me. How did she do this?

My facial features became softer, and I allowed my eyes to fill with tears as well.

I heard Josefine take a deep breath. What she did next had to cost her an outrageous force. She opened her arms, came closer and locked me in a hug. I could feel her trembling too, but she had decided to be there for me.

I didn't really know what to make out of this. Actually, I was supposed to be the one who took care of her, but apparently, Josefine seemed to be doing better that way as well.

I felt her warm breath on my ear. She was a little taller than me. I could feel her fingers moving slowly down my back.

"Everything will be fine. We'll get through this" Her words gave me a strange sense of comfort. Maybe it was because of the undertone in her voice. I had already noticed this at our first meeting. There was something in the way she spoke, the way she sounded, that had an incredibly calming influence. Jane was wrong.

Josefine was not the addict. She was the drug. She was everything one needed. She was strong even when she was falling apart. She helped even when she needed help herself. And that was no help, that was love. Josefine's way of giving love to everyone was enviable, and I couldn't wait to get to know more of her wonderful sides.

Josefine

After all, it was now clear why my psyche had had such terrible problems since the situation with Jane. God, I had to stop calling it a "situation". It was what it was. Harper was right once again. Jane had abused me. Sexually and emotionally. Even thinking about it felt like one of Orwell's thought crimes, but that was because my brain was manipulated by Jane. I had to come to terms with it, I had to accept it in order to be able to leave it behind me at some point.

It was also clear now why I had been so sensitive to physical contact lately. I had never really liked it, but although I had felt slightly uncomfortable when touching others, I had tended to not care. Never a big problem.

But just now, here on this hospital corridor, when I was holding Soleil in my arms, I felt much less inhibited.

Something about her was different, but I couldn't say exactly what yet. There was something about her that made her special, that made her extraordinary. Something... yeah, almost adorable.

And just this... something, prompted me to utter the words that now came out of my mouth. I was tired. I was confused, and I wanted nothing more than to be alone. It took me some time to understand what had happened today. And yet, I didn't want to be away from her. I wanted to be with her a little bit longer. There was something soothing about her smell, in a way that could not be explained with words.

"The offer for coffee is still standing," I whispered in her ear, careful not to speak too loudly, not to scare her, to protect her.

Soleil

I wanted to be alone, so I didn't understand why the words "Would love to" came out of my mouth.

There was something about Josefine that was special, compelling. I didn't feel like company, yet I didn't want to be without hers.

It was not the feeling of false politeness, of obligation, that moved me to accept her invitation. Much more, it was the way she asked. Her voice, the slight scent of rose emanating from the back of her neck, the way she held me. The fact that she was holding me. I remembered the last time we had touched. When I had not known- how she had reacted to our touch back then. Now she held me close, gave me security, because she somehow felt that I was about to lose all the ground I stood on.

It was the fact that she herself had to suffer so incredibly just now, and still wanted to be there for me, that made me not want to leave her.

I shouldn't trust her. Not after everything I had learned today, but she was different. She was a feeling that I was not able to put into words.

She seemed pure, good from the bottom of her heart. She was a feeling that, if I was completely honest with myself, I had never felt with Jane. There was something about her that screamed, "I'm not going to hurt you," and that was what attracted me to her so much.

I didn't know anyone else who exuded this feeling so purely. I knew many good and kind people, many who had given me this feeling in parts, but Josefine- I caught myself calling her Finchen in my mind, was the embodiment of this feeling.

As I expected, drinking coffee with her had been a good idea. After a while, we even managed to turn the topic into something normal. At a certain point, everything we said was no longer about Jane. She was the distraction I needed so badly right now, but oh dear, she wasn't just that. She was so much more, and the longer I listened to her talking, the more confident I became that I liked her. That I liked her profoundly, and to my own surprise I realized that I hadn't felt that way about Jane for a long time. I was still hurt, but being with Josefine, feeling her closeness, gave me a feeling that I had not felt in an awfully long time.

It was the feeling of being really wanted. To be wanted, for me, for the way I was, for the way I thought and spoke and existed. I felt seen.

Josefine had a way about her that made one feel special. In her presence, one felt comfortable, one felt validated. And she somehow managed to get excited about everything. She managed to make people feel admired without putting herself in an inferior position.

I liked the person I was when I was in her presence. That was also ultimately what led me to ask her *the* question; "I know this must sound incredibly inappropriate right now, and I would certainly understand if you said no, but I just can't not ask. I like the person you are, and I like myself when I'm with you. I have the feeling you are something very special, so... would you go on a date with me? "

I had the impression that the smile that played around her lips became even wider. "You like yourself because you are wonderful, and I would love to go on a date with you"

When she said these words, I had the feeling that from now on, everything would somehow get better. Maybe it was her, maybe it was myself, but I was suddenly filled with an incredible sense of optimism.

Josefine

The doorbell rang and my heart started pounding all the way up to my throat. I was afraid of doing something wrong. Actually, I knew I had nothing to be afraid of. Soleil was respectful and she liked me. She was charming, and not the kind of person who judged other people. I could relax, after all, that's what the rational half of me said. Still, I was jittery, and my hands were shaking. I was incredibly nervous, but in a positive way. I really wanted this date with Soleil to go well because I really fancied her. I would even go so far as to say that I had already fallen a little for her and her ways. I couldn't deny that I had a crush on her, but I also didn't have to. She and especially her smile were enchanting.

I had made an extra effort to dress up, but I didn't know what Soleil was wearing. I didn't want to embarrass her by being much more dressed up than she was. On the other hand, I didn't want to pretend that I didn't care what I looked like, especially in front of her. I wanted her to know that there wasn't a nonchalant bone in my entire body. I wanted her to know that this date- and her, were important to me. I wanted her to know that I was passionate and that I stood by it.

A small part of me was even particularly keen to emphasise the positive sides of me. A small and mean voice in the back of my head reminded me of the state Soleil had seen me in so far. At best, I had been tired, destroyed, broken. I had never been myself, she hadn't got to know me yet, not the real Josefine, not the enthusiastic and cheerful person, full of joie de vivre and love, that I was. And that little mean voice in my head whispered to me very quietly that I had to make an effort to be enjoyable now, otherwise Soleil would see me as a burden. Maybe she wouldn't hesitate to pursue a friendship with me, but she would no longer find me attractive. That voice was a rotten traitor, I knew that. Soleil wasn't perfunctory, but I gave in to the impulse and smiled a little wider than usual. I also let my appearance shine a little more. Shining for the sun that had just entered my flat.

She looked so incredibly beautiful. She wore her long blonde hair half-open and curled, gleaming in the light from my hall-way. She had pinned part of it up in a little knot at the back of her head. She was wearing a grey knitted dress and black tights. She had exactly matched the flair of my look.

She looked elegant, but not overdressed either, she looked normal, but in a compellingly charming way. When I looked at her, with that slightly shy look in her eyes, my heart gradually began to beat faster again. She was holding a bouquet of baby breath in her hand. It smelled so good when she gave it to me that it seemed surreal. I loved these flowers. With a smile on my lips, I took the bouquet and invited her in further. She had a scent about her that was wonderful, like a mixture of freshly mown grass on a warm summer's day mixed with the smell of orchids. When she entered, she gently put down her bag. The look in her beautiful blue eyes scanned my hall-way and the visible part of my living room. "Everything in here looks so cozy" she said, looking at me. These eyes, these ocean-blue eyes! I realised I was getting a little shy. "Thank you" I finally replied. There was a silence in the room because neither of us really knew what to say or do. It was as if there was something between us that we were both afraid would break if one of us said or did the wrong thing. I noticed a slight blush rising in my cheeks.

I just couldn't help it, I had to look at her again, her beautiful face with those perfectly shaped lips that I would love to kiss, the curve of her nose. She was just so incredibly pretty, and her freckles were driving me all the more mental. "Shall we go to the kitchen?" she asked and I nodded in agreement.

"Do you fancy some music?" I had a quiet hope that it was music that gave us both the jolt we needed to relax, we'd had such a pleasant and profound conversation sitting in the café. As she nodded to me in agreement, I switched on the kitchen radio. 'Est-ce que tu m'aimes?' by GIMS was playing, *how very fitting.*

It was a magical sight when Soleil simply started to dance. She was so self-confident, I really admired that about her.

I took a knife from the kitchen drawer and started to first slice and then dice the tomatoes and cucumber. While I did this, Soleil washed the head of salad. Every now and then I glanced over at her, she fascinated me! Her legs, the sweet smile, she was the embodiment of everything I had ever imagined, and now she was standing in my kitchen washing lettuce. When she had finished, I took the cabbage in my hand and started cutting it into pieces on the chopping board. "Josefine" Soleil exclaimed with a laugh, "what are you doing?"

"Well, I'm cutting the lettuce" I admitted, a little embarrassed.

"You don't chop salad" she pretended to lecture, "That's terrible!"

"To be honest, I've never done it any other way" I replied with a smile.

"A little odd, but somehow also quite cute" she replied with a grin, her deep blue eyes practically eating into mine. Her gaze was penetrating. I felt like she could look straight into my soul with her eyes.

It was like one of these romantic films that people said were unrealistic and would never happen in the real world; our eyes locked and now she was starting to blush as well. The moment seemed like half an eternity. I felt like I was drowning, in the best way imaginable. "So can I carry on?" I asked, acting puzzled.

"Of course!" she replied with an amount of benevolence in her voice that made me chuckle. She acted as if she was encouraging a child swimming for the first time. I loved her sense of humour, she was perfect, nothing short of perfect. While I continued to massacre the salad, Soleil took care of the dressing, still dancing around me to the music. I had been so focussed on not cutting my fingers that I flinched when two hands slowly wrapped around my waist from behind and carefully encircled my stomach. I felt my heart starting to beat faster as I felt her upper body nestle against my back. Jane's image briefly flashed through my mind, but I wouldn't let her take this moment away from me.

The moment I felt her warm breath on the back of my neck, it was all over for me. I slowly turned to face her, careful to stay in her arms. This time our eye contact lasted much longer. I looked down towards her and she looked up at me. I lost myself in her gaze, which was as deep as the pacific ocean, and savoured the moment. I felt like I could fly and fall kilometres deep at the same time. It was this moment that made me realise that this woman was worth everything. I was standing here, in her arms, looking into her eyes. *My life couldn't be better.*

Finally, I felt her grip on my waist tighten a little, catapulting me out of my trance state and back into reality. I took her waist in my hands, lifted her up and set her down on the countertop behind me. She took note of this with a sound of astonishment. Now I had to look up at her. My hand gently stroked her cheek and brushed a strand of hair behind her ear. My other hand was on her lower back, approximately at the level of her coccyx. Her fingers gently stroked my collarbone until she held my face in her hands. She slowly approached me, but before our lips could touch, she stopped. "Are we about to kiss?" she breathed, barely perceptible.

We were in such close proximity that I could not only hear her words, but feel them on my lips. "I'm all yours" was the last thing I uttered before she kissed me, and kissing was an understatement. It was magical, *she* was magical.

At first her mouth was gentle on mine, carefully exploring my lips, but then I slowly felt her tongue in my mouth. Her lips on mine became more demanding and I moulded my whole body against her. I could hardly bear the physical distance between us, she couldn't be close enough to me, and as if she had heard my thoughts, her hands pulled my body tighter so that not a single molecule could separate us. A firework of emotions exploded within me. I had never felt anything like what I had just felt. She softly groaned into my mouth; she seemed to like it just as much. My hand left her waist, stroking the back of her head, running through her beautiful honey-coloured hair, which was now loose as her topknot had come undone while dancing. She gently bit my lower lip. A sound escaped from my lips in response. The moments when I shared the best kiss of my life with her passed like seconds, and I never wanted it to end, this pleasant tightening in my stomach when her hands and mouth did these things to me, but eventually we slowly pulled away from each other.

I heard her breath, felt it gently on my nose.

As she slid off the counter, still with a slight blush on her face, and I started draping the plates with salad, Soleil switched off the music. After our kiss, the mood was no longer uncertain, like it was at the beginning, instead it was familiar, like the other day. While we ate, we talked about all sorts of things and I felt more free and understood than ever.

I also learnt a lot about Soleil that evening. She loved to debate as much as I did, had a soft spot for philosophy, and, even if this part wasn't really a new piece of information for me, was an absolute sunshine of a person. She had a magnificent soul. After dinner, we decided to watch a film. We sat on my couch together and I put the laptop on our legs. We were so close that my heart rate increased within seconds. When the film started, I felt her rest her head on my chest. I put my arms around her and our gazes met. I immediately had to start smiling again. She was so wonderful. We sat like that until about halfway through the film, but when it was time for the kissing scene, she carefully took my face in her hands and turned my head towards her. After Soleil had taken one look at me to make sure I was okay with it, her lips found mine. This kiss was different. She gently began to bite my lower lip before tracing a trail of kisses down to my collarbone. It felt beyond words. I heard her carefully close the laptop with one hand and set it aside, then her attention was completely mine.

She leant over me, pushing me back onto the couch until I was lying down. Her body weight gently pinned me into the cushions of the sofa. Her tongue teased the inside of my mouth. I gasped as my emotions seemed to overflow. And then there was this moment when we momentarily drew away from each other. Her face hovered just millimetres above mine. We both started to smile, I couldn't see it, but I felt it, she was so close to me. I felt this moment was indescribably intimate because it showed me how much happiness we could both feel from a kiss. It was as if a special bond had been forged between us in these seconds, as if a part of her soul had been transferred to me.

I placed my hand on her lower back and sat up. My legs wrapped around her hips and I pressed her against the back of the couch as we sat. My hands tightened around her neck. I nuzzled her collar, blowing kisses on her cheekbones. When she exhaled, there was an irrepressible murmur.

I started kissing Soleil's lips again. Our tongues brushed against each other. I stood up carefully and we stumbled towards the bedroom, continuing to kiss.

Carefully, one button at a time, she opened my blouse, and for every piece of skin that was revealed, she gave me a kiss. Now the lace of my olive-coloured bra was completely visible. Her fingers ran over my abs. I carefully took hold of her hips and lifted her up. I gently placed her on the bed and leant over her. She pulled me down towards her and after making sure she didn't mind, I took off her top as well. I kissed her décolleté, her stomach. Her arms resting on the pillow next to her head. I held them tight, hearing her inhale sharply.

She leaned towards me, her back formed into a hollow and I continued where we had left off.

After a while, I rolled to the side, my eyes fixated on her. I laid on my back and she turned onto her stomach to snuggle up to me.

I felt her warm skin on mine as a heated feeling spread through me.

"Am I your first choice?" Soleil whispered. "No" I replied. She looked at me, startled. I ran my hand through her hair. "If only you were my first choice, then there would be someone else I would feel that way about. You're not my first choice, and you never will be. You're my only choice!"

"I love you" were her last words before we fell asleep together.

True Events (author's note)

The story described in this book is based on true events, which are described and explained below.

Even though the three protagonists of this work are all of legal age, in reality there were only two children.

I invite you on a journey to the year 2020. There we meet Lilli (Josefine) and Fiona (Jane). The two know each other from school. They belong to different grades but were introduced to each other due to many of the same characteristics.

Lilli is 13 and Fiona is 14 years old. Every scene of the story that has the setting of the university took place like this, except for one, in the school of the two girls.

The scenes that take place at Josefine's home do not take place in Lilli's apartment, but in her room.

Lilli was always a friendly girl but was very insecure at the time being. She had no friends, and little social affiliation. Since she was different from most other children of her age. Since she had a far above-average intelligence, she was often excluded or teased. This made her already rather shy character very insecure and open to accepting everything that seemed to come close to love and acceptance of her personality in some form.

Fiona was Lilli's exact counterpart. She knew what she wanted and was not ashamed to be different. Although she was unique, she was therefore also perceived differently by her peers, which only reinforced her in the fact that she was something special. Also, she rarely entered into relationships for the sake of human relationships, but weighed what benefit she could derive from what interaction. However, Lilli was not aware of this at that time.

The core scenes, which revolve around Josefine's feelings as well as the description of the sexual abuse are the- admittedly unadorned- truth of what happened.

As mentioned earlier, a scene at school/university did not take place in real life, but in order to explain this properly, I will have to disclose further information to you. Hello, my name is Lilli Josefine Wettke and what you have just read is part of my personal story. Well, that was probably a surprise, I suppose, but one good thing is that I can finally stop talking about myself or my Alterego in the third person. That feels strange (if you don't believe me, just try it for yourself).

Okay, but joking aside. You are reading this part of the book because you are interested in the true events of my narrative. After all, I'm assuming that.

As I said, one of the situations described never took place like this in real life, and that is Jane's feigned suicide attempt. But why did I insert this scene then? I was just bored! Nope, not showing. During our "friendship" Fiona often, sometimes more, sometimes less obvious, told me that she was mentally unstable, and there was a chance that she would take her own life if I left her. This has led to the fact that for a period of more than a school year, almost every lesson, I had the picture in front of my eyes how one of the secretaries would rushingly enter the room and reveal to me that Fiona had taken her own life in a new way. What was a constant part of these horror visions was the fact that a letter was always found on her body, which attributed the complete blame for the situation to me. Sometimes she also stormed into my classroom with a drawn knife, screamed guilt in my face, and stabbed herself in front of my eyes. I had this vision several times, and it was equally painful every time. However, once I managed to throw myself between her and the knife, which, conversely, led to the fact that she stabbed me instead of herself. In a strange way, this was the most pleasant of these kinds of visions that I experienced at that time. The thematized letters are worthily represented in the said scene by the character Soleil, which I created in my head. Her existence has several backgrounds. She symbolizes in the parts of the book in which she interacts with Fiona, or in this case Jane, the emotional abuse that I had suffered at Fiona's hands until that fateful day of the sexual assault. Like Soleil, I was unable to understand what was happening to me at the time. Since this kind of abuse is also part of my story, I decided to pin this on the character dynamics between Jane and Soleil. In the relationship with Josefine, I chose Soleil as the character who embodied both the social burdens that I encountered when I decided to muster the courage in some places and to talk openly about what had happened to me. Let's just put it this way and call it by its name; a lot of the reactions I got were unprofessional, immature, and hurtful. Looking back, I can say that I was already more mature than one or the other adult at that time. At least in regard of such situations.

In the end of the story, however, the role of Soleil changes, to a character who also suffers, and becomes an important part of Josefine's life.

Again, Soleil is a humanization of two things. On the one hand, she is the emotionally intelligent and mature support that I would have liked very much at that time. Soleil treats Josefine in a way that I wish I had been treated by someone. On the other hand, she herself is broken and sad. In the scene, after everything has dissolved, we become eyewitnesses of how Josefine takes Soleil in her arms and comforts her. Here I am referring to a very specific characteristic of mine, of which I am admittedly no less proud. Even as a child or teenager, I was a person with a strong sense of justice, who, although not for herself, always stood up for others. Even today, I continue to try to embody this characteristic as much as possible. I am a person who likes to be there for others, and who is happy to make others happy. I didn't write this scene to give myself credit, but because I wanted to tell thirteen-year-old Lilli;

"Hey, you did a damn good job there. I'm proud of you!" I was broken myself at the time, but I never stopped taking care of others. This is a feature that I like.

If you enjoyed the book, or if you did not, if you have any questions or comments, then I would be happy if you let me know.

Feel free to leave me a direct message or a comment on Instagram (@written.by.lilli).

The real case

Lilli J Wettke aka. Josefine
date of birth 11.01.2007
date of crime: 16.10.2020
age while crime: 13 Jahre

Fiona K. aka. Jane
date of birth 08.09.2006
age while crime: 14 Jahre
(further information will be detained due to privacy reasons)

Acknowledgements

My first thanks goes to everyone who has supported me in some way or another.
In particular, I would also like to thank my friends. Those who stayed, thank you Phillip, thank you Julia, and those who I have met after, and who have accepted and loved me with all my problems and peculiarities from the very beginning. I love you guys! Thank you Isa, thank you Lena, thank you Alice (Alicia), thank you Theresa, thank you Tim, thank you Lana, thank you Julia, thank you Dora, thank you Inea, thank you Leonie (Niiku).
You deserve the saying "If life gives you gators, make Gatorade 🐊 🍹 "
I would also like to thank my wonderful L, as it has somehow become a tradition in my books in the meantime.
At this point I would like to quote myself, because I can't really express it better than in one of my (unsent) letters to you; You have back brought my ability to love. Not just simply to flirt, or to rave for someone, but to really, fully love. You made me a whole person again, because what is a human without the ability to love?
My final thanks go to the people who specifically supported me in writing this book. Many thanks to my wonderful editor Julia my photographer Greta and the people who follow my writing process on Instagram (@written.by.lilli). Thanks also to my favourite café @othello_kaffeebar. I owe the energy for about half of the scenes in this book to your Vanilla Chai Latte with cinnamon. Honestly, you guys are great!

About the author

Lilli J Wettke was born on January 11th 2007 in Trier.
She has published multiple novels, such as "Drenched- Love letters I wish I could send you" and "612- Encounters with a stranger".
In addition to having published her first novel at only fourteen years old, she can call herself an award-winning speaker. Alongside to her job as a karate teacher, she is interested in philosophy, psychology, poetry and physics. In her spare time, Lilli likes to be creative and devotes herself to art as well as reading, writing and spending time with her friends. She also likes to be informed and engaged politically.

Therefore, in this novel, her main goal is to attract attention. She has decided to share her personal story to give a voice to all victims, and to say: You are not alone!

You can find her on Instagram at @lilli.wettke and @written.by.lilli.